I0563916

A Simple Wedding in Bakersfield

By Elizabeth Bourgeret

The Bakersfield Series

DCT Publishing
St. Louis, MO
Printed in the United States of America

Author Photo & Front Cover Photo by
Steve Frank
Additional Artwork by Kylie Prestein

www.elizabethbourgeret.com
www.facebook.com/EBourgeret
@EBourgeret on Twitter and Instagram

ISBN 13: 978-0-9982866-9-3
ISBN 10: 09982866-9-9

Spoiler Alert!!!
Do not read this book unless you have read the other books in the Bakersfield Series. (Waiting for the Sun, Daddy's Girl and A Detour Home) Events and information presented in this novel will reveal outcomes of the plots from the previous books.

Other Books by Elizabeth Bourgeret

The Bakersfield Series:
Waiting for the Sun
Daddy's Girl
A Detour Home
A Simple Wedding in Bakersfield

Historical Fiction:
Captive Heart

Non-Fiction:
Pillow Talk: Connecting More Deeply to the One
You Love- One Question at a Time

Love Begins With You- Leading With Love Series

A Simple Wedding in Bakersfield

The Bakersfield Series

DCT PUBLISHING
St. Louis, MO

Trust in
the Lord with all
your heart and lean
not on your own
understanding;
Proverbs 3:5

Prologue

Evelynn St. Lawrence sat in the plush wingback chair in the dimly lit dressing room with her knees pulled up to her chest, her golden-yellow formal gown spilling about her like a smooth velvety liquid. Her perfectly manicured hands rested in her lap and she didn't even attempt to stop the tears from ruining her mascara.

Big, wet snowflakes dotted the landscape and began to accumulate on the empty parking lot of the Bakersfield Theatre. The sun was fighting the losing battle with the grey, snow-laden clouds.

"Today was supposed to be my wedding day…"

Chapter One

"Oh, honey!! It's so beautiful!" Gillian leaned across Gwen's legs to see the shining diamond on Evelynn's hand.

"It was his grandmother's. He had it sent here and just got it back from the jewelers where he sized it for me."

"Awwww!" The three ladies swooned at the beautiful engagement ring.

Evelynn St. Lawrence, the Executive Director of the local Fine Arts Centre, leaned back in her lawn chair and watched the glow from the campfire bounce off the perfectly cut antique diamond. Her dark hair was pulled back into a low ponytail that hung down over her shoulder.

Gwen, the Artistic Director for the Centre, sat beside her. They had been friends for many years and opened the Fine Arts Centre to offer classes in the arts and to produce local dance, theatre and art productions for Bakersfield, Arkansas and the surrounding counties. She wore her straight blonde hair down her back and held it all in place by dropping a *Real People, Real Lives* ball cap on top of her head. "His grandfather sure had good taste!" she laughed.

Evelynn blushed slightly, "Dave did enlarge the center diamond, he said."

"It's just beautiful," Gillian repeated her sentiment. She was one of the dance and art instructors at the Centre. She too donned a ballcap to cover her short dirty blond locks. She tucked a loose strand behind her ear and asked, "So, how are the wedding plans coming?"

The campfire crackled and popped like it was attempting to be a part of the conversation. Gwen would poke at the embers on the logs every once in a while to make sure the flames continued to produce warmth and light to their little party as the sun was deciding to set.

"Pretty good," Evelynn said thoughtfully. We are trying to throw the whole thing together in a few months so as not to disrupt the Centre's schedule."

Gwen looked over at Gillian and smirked, "Isn't she sweet, to not abandon us for too long?"

Gillian laughed, "Nicer than I am!   I completely left you guys for a while there!"

"That was a bit of a different situation," Evelynn recalled.   "Who would have thought something like that could happen in sleepy ol' Bakersfield.

"I won't forget *that* holiday season any time soon!" Gwen added.

"You?"   Gillian chortled, "I still have nightmares..."

"Ms. G!"   A loud voice interrupted their thoughts. "Mr. Nick say to ask you if you want the marshmallows now or not."

"Shurita!" Gwen stood up and reached her arm out behind her prompting a rare embrace. "I didn't see you earlier."

"I was inside mostly, tryin' ta get away from these mosquitos. Lawd, they like to tear me up." She flapped her arms about, swinging at any would be tiny attackers. Her black hair was pressed straight and came down to her shoulders. She wore a scarf as a headband, tied in a bow at the top. "Tyrell s'posed to be here, but he cancelled."

Gillian raised her eyebrows, "Cancelled or didn't bother to show up?"

"Now Ms. G, don't be like dat... he okay."

Gillian shrugged, "I can't help it. You're one of my own. I don't want him to hurt you."

"I know Momma Bear, I feel ya..."

Evelynn interjected, rescuing the teenager, "I'm ready for marshmallows, anyone else?" She winked at Shurita and smiled.

Shurita laughed, "You sho right, Ms Evie. Thank you for dat. You know Ms. G was jus gettin' started," Shurita turned and walked away from the row of ladies, laughing under her breath. "Imma grown woman and she out here bein all protective and stuff..."

The women laughed. Gillian shook her head. "That girl. She's pretty amazing."

The other two nodded.

"But back to the wedding..."

"Babe?" A masculine voice was heard coming from the back porch. The women turned and looked at each other trying to figure out who belonged to the voice. "Babe, where are the hotdog buns?"

Gwen nodded and raised her hand and mouthed the word "Me."

She stood up and started toward the house, but Nick Penn called again from the porch, "Found 'em!"

Gwen turned back around to go back to her lawn chair beside the fire.

They were in the back yard of former television star, Nick Penn. He had built a fire pit a few yards away from the pool and just finished adding a stone patio around the bricked, sunken stone pit. The men were inside boasting of their victories while the women chatted around the fire.

The sun was turning the sky shades of pink as it crept closer and closer to the horizon. The kids, varying in age, were inside watching a movie and it was a heavenly, peaceful evening for friendships.

It wasn't long before the men made their way to the stone patio, each carrying a tray filled with campfire goodies.

The ladies scooted over to allow their men-folk to sit between them. Tom opened a lawn chair and grabbed the cushion from a large plastic trunk that edged the far side of the patio. "Anyone else need a cushion?" he called out.

Both Nick and Dave nodded. "Since the women didn't bother to set up chairs for us, yeah,

I'll need one," Dave teased as he slipped over to kiss Evelynn on the top of her head.

"And we're in there slaving over the food..." Nick attempted.

"And watching baseball..." Gwen cocked her eyebrow.

Nick laughed and conceded, "There might have been a little baseball playing in the background."

"Hello..." a voice came from the porch.

"Oh hey! You made it!" Nick called back to the couple coming down the back steps to join them.

Gwen stood up to greet the newest guests.

"James, glad you could make it!" Nick clasped his hand. "You remember Gwen?"

James leaned in and hugged her. "Of course," he leaned conspiratorially toward Nick, "This is the one I have to butter up so we can get you your new Harley, right?"

Nick threw his head back and laughed. "I might have to get us each one!"

"Oh yeah? Let's talk, brother!" James shook his hand again and laughed. "Gwen, Nick, I want you to meet Nina Black."

"Hi, Nina, welcome."

"I thought that was you," Gillian came away from the fire and hugged the dark haired woman. "It's so nice to see you." She turned to Gwen and Nick to clarify, "Ms. Black has had a few of my kids in her history classes."

"Come on over," Nick gestured toward the fire.

"Did Danni come with you?" Gillian asked.

James nodded, "She's inside with Shurita."

"Oh, good, good," Gillian nodded. "She was hoping she would be here."

The four couples sat around the fire and followed the conversation wherever it led. A lot of theatre talk, some talk of fishing and future plans, talk of yesterdays...

"And there he was... picture this, the whole Greek god thing... one foot on a boulder and hands on his hips," Dave Ripke stood up to give an example of the pose he was referring to. "...rays of light coming from the back of his head, wearing some cut off jeans and a Dukes of Hazzard t-shirt," he paused to stick out his chest and shake his imaginary long flowing locks. "Yeah, that... and we became friends. Ya know, I showed him all my moves, put him in front of all the right people..." Dave made a muscle with his arm and kissed his bicep.

Nick Penn meanwhile was laughing so hard along with everyone else, shaking his head and shielding his face with his hand on his forehead.

Nick struggled to catch his breath, "Yeah, it went something like that. Hey, thanks for not leaving me alone at those summer camps, bud. You've made me the man I am today."

Dave laughed and saluted, "My best man, everybody!"

More logs were added to the fire...

"And so he was walking me to my front door, and suddenly he broke out into song," Evelynn was saying. "He was dancing around me and singing that Beach Boys song, uh... uh..."

"Really? You forgot already?" Dave teased her.

Evelynn was humming the tune in her head searching for the title, "Wouldn't It Be Nice... and he saying stuff like, 'we wouldn't have to wait so long' and 'we could spend the night together'... " Evelynn put her hand to her chest. A laugh bubbled up inside her and demanded to come out before she could continue, "And then..." she giggled, "And then he said, 'So, would you?' and I thought," she covered her face with her hand, blushing, "I can't believe I'm saying this... I thought he meant... you know... come inside... stay the night together..."

Dave laughed and added to her embarrassment, "Such a forward woman. She only wants me for my body."

"But no, that was his marriage proposal. When I paused and didn't answer, he said, 'I'm serious, you wanna get hitched?'"

Dave was nodding as if he was the most romantic man alive, "Don't steal that one boys, it's totally my line." He picked up and kissed the back of her hand, which was already laced with his.

And later into the evening...

"I was called to this house. Gorgeous house. It was from, like the 1700's, I think," James looked at Nina for confirmation, "And they took me out to this barn." He let go of Nina's hand so he could properly tell the story. He leaned forward on his knees with his hands spread out in front of him as if he were ready to catch a beach ball. "In this barn, I kid you not, they pull this heavy canvas drape off... and there sits... in mint condition a 1927 Horch. I mean, the original upholstery, the chrome, the motor, everything was there. These German-made beauties came from this guy August Horch. He used to work for the popular Benz company..." everyone nodded at the finally familiar name, "And Horch eventually started his own company... late eighteen hundreds... amazing piece of machinery."

A series of "oooh's" and "aaahh's" responded at the appropriate times. "I ended up giving the lady twice as much as she asked for because she just didn't realize what she had. It was her husband's Sunday car, she called it. He would only drive it to church and back."

"Where was this?" Tom asked.

"A little town called Beaufort, South Carolina. Great place. Didn't you think?" he turned the question to Nina.

"Oh yes, we could have stayed there a couple more weeks and I would have been fine with that. So much history there."

Nina nudged James in the arm, "You didn't tell them the best part."

James looked at her, confused.

"About the car..." James still looked at her blankly. She rolled her eyes and directed her comments to the ladies. "When he opened the trunk of the car, inside was a box full of this couple's history. There was a photo album, a few embroidered handkerchiefs..."

"A cup and saucer made from china or something..." James added.

"And a wedding dress. It was wrapped in paper and then in plastic. It is beautiful. I'm going to have it cleaned and see if the museum wants it."

"That is fascinating!" Gwen commented.

"Did the woman even know they were there?"

"James called them when we got home and found it, but they said we could donate or keep whatever we found."

"I think the woman was getting ready to go to a home, or something," James filled in the missing piece.

"So that's your place outside of town, then? The Barn?" Dave asked, changing the subject slightly.

James nodded, "It is."

"I love that Stingray you've got on the turnstyle out front. Really a nice piece."

James searched his memory bank, "She's a sixty-six, I believe. She was little more than a shell when I got her."

Dave nodded respectfully, "Nice work. What's something like that go for?"

James, smiled and chuffed, "That baby, will go for about seventy-eight to ninety-four thousand."

"Whoo!" Dave shook his hand as if he touched something hot. "Put me down for two!"

James tipped his head back and laughed. He stood and reached across the fire pit to shake his hand, "You got it, brother."

As the night drew on and the kids were getting sleepy or bored with their movie selection, Shurita and Danni came out to join the adults. They pulled up two chairs just outside the circle as the others made room for them if they chose to "actually join" them.

Gillian asked Danni, "Where is Nate tonight?"

Danni curled her feet up on the chair and leaned her head against Shurita's shoulder. "He already had other plans," she answered sleepily.

Gillian nodded in response and it took Shurita less than ten seconds to chime in. "So why you ain't gonna give Danni a hard time?" She pursed her lips and cocked her head to the side.

Gillian nodded again, "My sincerest apologies," she began, her words heavy with sarcasm. "Danni, did Nate *really* have plans tonight or did he just not bother to show up?" Gillian raised her eyebrows at her almost grown former foster child, as if asking, *How was that*?

Danni laughed, "He really did have plans, Miss G."

Little Erin, Gwen's adopted eight-year old, came out and crawled into Nick's lap. "I'm sleepy."

Gwen leaned over and patted her leg, "Okay sweetie, we'll be leaving soon."

And just then, three girls came screaming from the house jarring all the adults to attention.

Not too far behind them was five-year old Ethan, chasing the girls with his plastic pirate sword.

Tom looked over at Gillian, "I think that's our cue."

Gillian laughed, agreeing. She uncrossed her legs and stood up as the four running children came sweeping by.

"Not around the fire," Tom scolded.

Everyone started to stand up, stretch and push their chairs back.

Gillian hugged Gwen and Evelynn, and made her way to Nina. "It was nice to finally meet you James," Gillian hugged him as well.

"Likewise."

"Okay! My monsters and pirates, let's clean up and get home!"

"Imma go home wit Danni, okay?"

Gillian nodded. "See you at church tomorrow, then?"

"We'll be there."

"Okay, be safe. I love you." She kissed Shurita on the head. "And I love you." She kissed Danni on the head.

"Yeah, yeah, we're out too. I'm gonna take her home and then come back here to crash," Dave said to Nick.

"Me casa tu casa," Nick smiled and patted Dave on the back. He put Erin on her feet and reached out to hug Evelynn as they headed toward Dave's car.

Nick shook James' hand, "Thanks for coming out. Don't be a stranger."

James bobbed his head, "This not working all the time and hanging out with friends is something I might be able to get used to. He laughed and put his arm around Nina.

"Told you, Dad," Danni chided him.

"You did, child, you did." He kicked the leg of her chair, bouncing her. "C'mon kiddo, let's get home."

She and Shurita moved in slow motion, disappointed to have to move at all.

Finally it was just Nick, Gwen and Erin left at the house.

"Want me to stay and help clean up?"

Nick wrapped her in his arms and buried his face into her neck. "I want you to stay here forever."

She scrunched her face and giggled. Her body got goosebumps as his lips tickled her neck. She pulled away from him and kissed his nose. "We aren't even engaged."

"Then I can have you?"

"After the perfect wedding."

"Do you want a Cinderella wedding?"

She pulled back, pausing, not having really thought about it. "Do you?"

He smiled and kissed her. "I want what you want."

"So I can have whatever kind of wedding I want?"

"You can."

"Seventeen bridesmaids, three junior brides, two flower girls..."

He silenced her with a kiss. "Whatever you want. But then... I get to keep you?"

A smile spread across Gwen's face. "For the rest of your life."

He kissed her lips, her nose, her cheeks and came back for a deep kiss but, right then a small child had wormed her way between them.

"Me too, Momma..."

Gwen laughed, "You too?" she reached down and groaned as she picked Erin up in her arms. "You need kisses too?" Gwen kissed her face a few times. "Nick, she said she needed kisses."

Nick joined in, and soon, Erin was covered in tiny little kisses by two grown-ups that loved her, and each other deeply.

"I can't wait to make us a family," Nick whispered.

Chapter Two

As an engagement gift for the new couple, Nick Penn orchestrated a weekend getaway to Memphis, TN. He purchased tickets for *Les Miserable*, which Dave slept through, the girls wept through and Nick tried to figure out how it could be produced at Bakersfield.

The next afternoon, he dropped the girls off at the exclusive *Frenchman's Daughter Wedding Boutique...*

Gwen slouched in a low back velvet chair wearing a blood red satin gown that draped itself around her beautiful dancer's body. She held a tall champagne glass in her right hand and looked like she'd just stepped from the pages of the *Great Gatsby.*

A matronly woman in her late forties refilled her champagne glass from behind the chair. "That dress is stunning on you, ma'am," she stated.

Gwen looked over her shoulder and smiled, loving the attention and the dress selection. "Thank you. I think it might be a little too red for a wedding."

"Oh, no, that's the latest thing these days. The brides are wearing reds and blacks and every color in between."

Gwen sat up tall in her chair when Evelynn emerged from behind the wall of mirrors and stood on the platform to view herself.

She wore a cream colored version of the satin gown Gwen wore. "Oh, honey! That is gorgeous!!" Gwen gasped.

Evelynn turned away from the mirror and scrunched up her face. "Makes my boobs look saggy."

Gwen dropped her head and laughed. Noticing her own neckline, she added, "Yeah, I guess you're right. We'd need to adjust that somehow." She stood and brought Evelynn her champagne. "Something more traditional then?"

Evelynn shrugged. "Yeah, I guess. I just don't like these sheath dresses for a wedding."

"That's okay. But just so you know, it looks beautiful on you."

"Yours looks amazing on you, too. Maybe you should wear that for your wedding," Evie suggested.

"It's not a bad idea. I do like them." Gwen stood on the platform beside her best friend and looked back over her shoulder at herself in the mirror. "We'll keep it in mind."

"Ummm... I'm sorry... Ma'am?" Evelynn called out to the woman on standby. "Could we maybe see some items a little more traditional?"

"Of course. I'll bring you a selection to your dressing room." She nodded and slipped away.

"Here... take a sip. You look so tense. This is supposed to be a fun day." Gwen guided the beverage to Evie's lips.

"It is fun. I love our little Memphis getaway. But... these prices... I just... I can't justify...."

"Don't worry about that just now. We're just seeing what style you like and what fabrics you like."

"Yeah, but... I... these dresses are so expensive! The cheapest one was $8,000!"

"Now, don't you worry about that..."

"If you're planning on paying for...."

"No... no, it's not that... I..."

"I'm not spending this fortune for a dress I'm only going to wear once and that will probably end up in the theatre's costume closet!"

Gwen burst out laughing. The saleswomen burdened with lace, petticoats and hangers wafted by to get Evelynn set up in the dressing room.

"Evie... this is a most sacred day I know. Your wedding is special and should be everything you want it to be... but... our area of expertise is... productions. Theatre. Things aren't always what they look like on the stage from the audience's perspective. Your wedding, really is... another production." Gwen scrunched her face hoping that she wasn't offending. As there was no critical look from her best friend, she continued, "And if we treat it as such, we will save a fortune. So keep trying on your 'costumes'," Gwen air-quoted the word, winking "...then we will go back to the theatre and re-create it... Centre Style..."

Evelynn stared at her best friend letting the plan sink in and a grin spread across her face. "You sly fox."

Gwen shrugged, "I'm just the best maid of honor ever, that's all."

Gwen twirled in an off the shoulder bridesmaid dress waiting for Evelynn to appear in her next choice.

Evelynn smiled as she peeked out from behind the mirrors. The white lace mermaid style had a heart shaped décolleté, long lacey sleeves and thousands of sequins and pearls sewn on.

"Oh! Evie!" Gwen gasped. "That is amazing! Do you see yourself?"

Evelynn scooted toward the center of the mirror, and smiled. "I think this one is my favorite so far," she blushed.

"It's magnificent!"

Evelynn turned so she could see herself from all sides. She couldn't contain her smile. "I feel so elegant."

"You *look* so elegant! Dave won't know what to do with himself!"

"He probably wouldn't even notice. He'd be happy if I showed up in a burlap sack. Just as long as I show up!" Evelynn laughed nervously.

"How could he not notice how beautiful you are... this is ... I mean... this is beautiful!"

Evelynn looked down at the price tag that dangled under her arm and gulped, "It's in the double digits!!!"

"Then don't rip anything!!"

"Right, I'm going on to the next one." She gingerly turned to exit but stopped to ask, "What time are we meeting the boys?"

Gwen stepped down from the platform and checked her phone. "We're good. We have about another hour before we meet them for dinner."

"Okay... on to the next one..." Evelynn took a few more steps but popped her head back around the mirror and whispered, "This one is my favorite."

"Take pictures!" Gwen whispered back.

Evelynn just rolled her eyes. "You're so bad..."

Just as Gwen was filtering through the rack of bridesmaid dresses deciding which one to try on next, Nick Penn walked into the salon with his hands covering his eyes.

"Is everybody decent?" he called out.

Gwen smiled at her boyfriend and answered, "We are."

Nick peeked through his fingers, "Dangit."

Gwen laughed and wrapped her arms around his waist and reached up for a kiss, letting him know that his presence is not unwelcome.

"Hello beautiful." He pulled her into a tight embrace.

"That makes me feel so special when you say stuff like that." She laid her head against his chest.

"Well, I mean it."

She leaned back to look up at him. "What are you doing here? I thought we weren't supposed to see you for another hour."

"Yeah, well, turns out that we aren't really the cigars and bourbon type of guys after all.."

"I can't say that I'm disappointed in your discovery. So what have you been doing?"

"Well, since we're in Memphis, and Dave has never been to…"

And, as if on cue, Dave sashays his way into the parlor wearing an Elvis wig and oversized rhinestone-studded sunglasses singing, "hunka-hunka burnin' love".

"Uh…yeah. So… Graceland," Nick smirked.

Gwen fought to stifle the laugh that was begging to escape.

"Hey Gwen!" Dave called out, shooting his finger guns in rapid succession as he inched toward her.

Gwen giggled, "Don't you look cute."

Dave, not missing a beat, whipped off his sunglasses and bobbed his eyebrows, "Shpank you, shpank you very much."

Gwen burst out laughing while Nick rolled his eyes. Gwen looked up at him.

"It's not really that funny after the twenty-seventh time."

"Aw, c'mon…. Dude, that's gonna be funny way into the thirties, I'm tellin ya. Hey, where's my bride, I suddenly have inspiration for how we're going to paint our living room…"

"She's in the back, changing. But just a head's up, she's not a fan of the gold ceilings…"

"How does she feel about..." Dave cocked his one eyebrow, "... animal print?" He swung his arm in a circle and struck an iconic Elvis pose.

And it was then that Evelynn slipped out from behind the mirrored wall to reveal the latest gown. Her audience gasped as she smiled down at them and spun completely around.

"I feel like a..."

"Is that what you're gonna wear?" Dave blurted out.

Nick slapped his hand to his face, embarrassed for his friend.

Dave, not even noticing the girls dropped jaws, stepped back and tapped his best friend on the arm, "Dude... dude... you know what that reminds me of?"

Gwen tried to interrupt, "Cinderella?"

Dave scrunched his face, like that was the dumbest answer ever, "No. That... that Barbie doll that sat on the back of my grandma's toilet? You know what I'm talkin' about? It was crocheted with like yarn and stuff and if you lifted her dress there was a roll of toilet paper hidden under there. You remember?"

Nick apologized with his eyes. He opened his mouth to speak but no words could remedy the situation. He turned Dave around and began escorting him from the room.

"I'm uh... sorry... yeah... no filter on this one..." Nick rolled his eyes.

"What? Tell me you don't see that!" Dave defended, as he was lead from the room.

"So... yeah, dinner then?" Nick looked to Gwen.

Gwen's lips pursed together and raised her eyebrows in disapproval, as she nodded as her answer.

When the room was deathly quiet once more, she covered her mouth and dared to glance up at the toilet paper bride.

All Evelynn could do was roll her eyes... "Yep.... That's the man I'm spending the rest of my life with..." and she sighed heavily and turned back toward the dressing room.

Way off in the distance they heard the front door of the salon open with a chime, and Nick's voice, "Elvis has left the building."

The two couples left the Peabody Hotel feeling overly full from dinner.

"Nick, you have spoiled us completely. Thank you so much for ... everything!" Evelynn leaned forward to link her arm with his.

"It really is my pleasure. You guys don't get to leave Bakersfield very often, so I thought..."

"It really is so sweet of you."

Nick patted the arm that rested in the crook of his elbow. "Hey, we're practically family."

Evelynn stole a glance at her best friend who occupied Nick's other arm and saw that she was quietly beaming.

"Hey, here's an idea," Dave stepped in front of the threesome and walked backwards, "Instead of going to Beale Street where it's going to be all noisy, how bout let's take a carriage ride? My treat?"

Evelynn smiled, "I would love that."

Dave held out his hand, which she gladly accepted, "My lady..."

They walked across the street to the selection of large carriages hooked up to beautiful white horses just waiting for hire.

"You guys wait here. I got this." Dave winked and stepped forward to speak with a man wearing a black, silk top hat. They spoke in low tones until Dave shouted, "What? You've got to be kidding me! I don't need a ride to California!"

"Dave..." Nick cautioned.

Dave looked back over his shoulder and frowned. "Right, right... I got this..." He pulled his wallet from his back pocket but not before uttering slightly under his breath, "... shyster."

The horses clip-clopped along making a rhythmic backdrop for the late summer evening joyride.

Gwen leaned her head on Nick's shoulder and closed her eyes, allowing her other senses to take charge. She could smell the vendor's candied pecans, the sweat from the horses... the breeze would bring just the slightest hint of the flowers that decorate the front of a hotel. She could hear the fountains and in her mind's eye saw them dancing and splashing about through colored lights.

"You really did look pretty today." Dave spoke softly.

Gwen opened one eye slightly to see Evelynn slide down in her seat to put her head on Dave's shoulder.

"Thank you."

"No, I mean it... I... just... don't know how to say stuff... and... you know."

Evelynn looked up at his face and smiled. It melted his heart and he wanted to hold her forever.

"You are... uh... different from anyone I've ever met," he cleared his throat. "I mean, you're so beautiful and I can't believe you are with me. Hell, I don't even want to sleep with you... I mean, I do... but I... I mean, I can... I want to ... uh... wait. You know?"

Gwen and Nick did their best not to laugh at his attempt, rough as it may be; it was a sincere attempt to verbalize his love. They became very still as they struggled to "disappear" in the cozy carriage.

Evelynn sat up and cupped Dave's face in her hands to turn it toward her. She smiled softly and said, "Thank you. That means so much to me."

Dave shrugged and attempted to turn away. But she held him and kissed his lips. "I know that my life... is completely different than the life that you're used to. And I hope that you never grow tired of me and long for your old life..."

Dave attempted to interrupt but she continued, "But it speaks volumes to me that you are willing to come into my world and that you recognize that I couldn't fit into yours. I am sorry if this is uncomfortable for you..."

"It's not. Well, I mean, kinda... especially when you kiss me like that, but hey, it's cool."

He laughed and was relieved to see the blush cross her cheeks along with a smile. "I love making you smile."

She tried to pull her hands back to cover her smile, but he took them in his hands instead. "Yeah, that smile." He leaned in to kiss her.

He pulled away from her and puffed his cheeks, blowing out air. "I might need you to scoot over there for a minute... "

She laughed and attempted to put space between them but he wrapped his arm around her and pulled her back against him. "I can take it. I don't want you so far away from me."

She smiled and tucked her nose under his chin; and despite the warm evening, they stayed cuddled together.

The two couples were quiet for the remainder of the romantic carriage ride, but love silently swirled around them.

Chapter Three

The Bakersfield Fine Arts Centre was relatively quiet for the next couple weeks as they waited for the fall season to kick off. As of right now, though, the Centre, which was the hub of Bakersfield for dance, theatre, and art classes, not to mention the finest local-talent theatre productions in three states, is being used as Wedding Central.

Betty came into her office and took one look at her desk and wondered where she was going to work today. There were samples of lace and satin draped over mounds of wedding magazines, brochures and... is that a cake platter?

Evelynn came breezing into the main office from her personal office, cheeks full and a chocolaty rim around her lips.

"Oh Betty," she attempted to speak, "I know chocolate isn't the usual choice for wedding cake, but try this!"

Before Betty could even respond, much less think of responding, Evelynn shoved half of a ball of cake into her mouth.

Evelynn raised her eyebrows, "Heavenly, right?"

Betty nodded, choosing not to add words so as to savor the baked confection.

"I don't know how I'm going to decide!" Evelynn walked over to Betty's desk and gingerly, with her pinky fingers slid the slippery material off the plastic lid of the assortment of cake balls for Evelynn to choose from. She licked her index fingers, but then stopped. "I should stop eating these."

Betty laughed. "I think maybe you should. From the looks of your face, you've been at it a while. Have you eaten any real food?"

Evelynn laughed and went over to a large oval mirror, and wiped the rim of her lips. "I wasn't expecting so much! They just arrived this morning from the confectioner we talked to in Memphis. This is the second tray," she said pointing back to Betty's desk. "Gwen and I finished off the other one. She rolled her eyes, "Oh, so good..."

Betty cocked her one eyebrow, and using her best maternal tone, "You'd better slow down or you won't be able to fit into your wedding dress."

Evelynn smiled and hugged the matriarch of the Centre. "I've got that covered," she kissed her cheek, "I haven't even made the dress yet!"

Gwen walked into the office and stopped short when both women turned to look at her. She literally looked like the cat who ate the canary... if it had been chocolate. "What?" she uttered with chocolate sputtering from her mouth. She laughed, embarrassed and reached up to cover her mouth. "Oh, I'm so disgusting! Sorry 'bout that," she laughed.

"Uh-huh," Betty's eyebrow went up again, "Partners in crime..." She shook her head.

"In my defense... I mean, have you tried these?" Gwen came to hand Betty a perfectly round piece of cake.

She lifted her hand in front of her mouth, "I've had the pleasure, yes."

Gwen shrugged, "See?"

Evelynn leaned in at that moment and spoke low to Betty, "We haven't made her dress either."

"And, in all fairness, I'm getting married next."

"Oh are you now?" Betty challenged Gwen. "He's proposed, has he?"

Gwen looked away sheepishly, "Well, no... but he has strongly indicated that we will be a family soon."

"We should all get married at the same time. You, me and Gillian!" Evelynn burst out. "Wouldn't that be fun?"

Gwen went over to hug her best friend. "That would be amazing and I would be so happy to stand up there with you and Gill, but..." she pulled back to arm's length. "This is YOUR day. And like Betty has mentioned," she tossed Betty a sour look, "I am still ringless."

"And my daughter is waiting one more year... as of this past weekend. She and Tom have everything pretty well mapped out.

Evelynn pouted. "We've done everything else together except our first marriages, and look how those turned out!" The two women giggled and pulled Betty into their embrace.

"Well good riddance to those two. They obviously didn't know what they had."

Gwen kissed Betty's head and released her. "You never met Carlos, did you, Betty?"

She shook her head.

Gwen leaned back on one of the desks, "He was a smooth talker."

"So handsome," Evelynn added.

"And that accent..." Gwen allowed herself a moment to recall, and then her face scrunched up. "But what a jerk!"

Evelynn leaned against a bookcase and closed her eyes, "But oh, how he could dance..."

Betty looked at Gwen for answers.

"He was our Latin dance teacher when we went through our "ballroom" phase," Gwen air-quoted the word. "That was waaaaay before our visions of having our own dance studio. But, he really was amazing. So smooth. He set his sights on Evie that first night, I think."

"What happened, if you don't mind my asking?" Betty scooped up the remnants of fabric from her chair and sat down to listen.

"He was a bum. He was all talk. Nothing underneath."

Evelynn looked down at her feet. "He lied to me. He cheated on me. He stole from me..." she shook her head.

"Why did you stay with him for so long?" Betty queried further.

Evelynn shrugged and stared off into space. She shook her head again, "Must have been the sex," she said matter-of-factly.

Gwen spit out her cake and nearly choked as laughter shook her body. Betty just closed her eyes and dropped her head down, finally knowing more than she cared to.

Evelynn looked up and blushed slightly realizing her thoughts came out of her mouth. "It's true," she laughed. "If we weren't dancing we were... you know... and if not that, he wasn't around." She finally covered her face and laughed. Gwen was beside herself in giggles and Betty... sweet Betty just looked up at the ceiling. "I don't know what you're gonna do with them, Lord.... I just can't... even..." they could hear her whisper, but knew that laughter was just under the surface.

They snickered a bit longer but then the smile left Evelynn's face as her thoughts turned inward. "I don't know. I guess I was afraid that maybe he would be the only one that would love me. Like, I'm not good enough for anyone else, you know?" She glanced over at the two ladies who sat quietly and listened. "We met in our late twenties?" She looked at Gwen for confirmation. Gwen nodded. "He was my first. So, by that time, I thought, I mean, I think we both thought we were the ugly duckling theatre nerds and it would just be us."

Gwen nodded, remembering. "We had convinced ourselves we were going to be cat ladies, with the most awesome libraries of both books and music."

Evelynn smiled at the memory. "I knew what he was doing, and I just let him. I knew it was wrong, and near the end, I didn't even like him. But every time I decided that I was going to leave..." she shook her head staring at nothing in particular, "It's like he knew, and he would be so sweet, and so attentive. And I'd end up giving him one more chance. Maybe I could love him enough for both of us. Maybe I'm not giving him the right *kind* of love." She took in a deep breath, "I just couldn't understand what I was doing wrong. Why couldn't he love me and stay faithful to me?" She wasn't asking for answers, but Betty could tell that the questions still haunt her. "I would have stayed with him forever if he would have just come a little my way... Even though the sad times out weighed the good times, I would have stayed..."

The room got quiet and still, no one knowing what to say until Gwen broke the silence.

"Aren't you glad you called me and we decided to open the Centre?" She squealed and ran over hugging her best friend, bending their bodies from side to side like a young tree in the wind. "I love you so much, Evie. I am glad that we made it through our mistakes and we have become better for it."

"Amen to that," Betty said.

"All the more reason we should get married at the same time." Evelynn nudged Gwen.

"Here, have some cake..." Gwen shoved a cake ball into her mouth.

Dave pulled up to Evelynn's house and got out of the car. She was ready and met him at the door. He reached up the two inches he lacked on her five foot eleven frame, kissed her and smiled at her.

"What?"

He shrugged, "What? Nothing." He shrugged again. "What have you got there?" he asked nodding his head at her plastic container.

She smiled. "You said we were going someplace special for a picnic, so I made you some peanut butter cookies."

"Really? I love those! Those are really like... my favorite! My aunt makes them every Christmas and I swear she never makes enough."

Evelynn giggled at him. "I know. I do listen when you talk, you know."

Dave blushed and grinned. He looked down at his feet then stuck out his elbow for her to grab on to. He escorted her to the passenger side of his leased Ford Tempo and opened the door. She slid inside and waited for him to close the door.

When he settled into the driver's seat, she asked, "When are you going to send for your things from California? Aren't you getting tired of driving around in this rental?"

Dave shrugged and chuffed, "It's nicer than the car I had there."

Evelynn furrowed her brow, "But don't you have to get things settled there? Like close your condo and pack your things? Won't you need the rest of your camera equipment?"

Dave Ripke was the camera man for the hit television show *Real People, Real Lives* that starred his best friend, Nick Penn. But Dave had never been very good about taking care of business. Sure, he usually paid his bills on time and those things, but it was easy for him to dismiss other responsibility. He hadn't even thought of having to leave Arkansas to go back to California. It hadn't even crossed his mind that he would have to completely end his West coast life.

He wanted this move, and he wanted to get married and he looked forward to spending the rest of his days in the very same town he'd made fun of only months ago, but actually completing the tasks to make it all happen, that was another story.

"Why do you want to keep paying rent if you aren't planning on going back?" A moment of panic slipped through Evelynn's veins. "You haven't changed your mind, have you?"

Dave looked over at her as he was driving, going back and forth from the road to her anxious face. "No... Oh, Babe, no! Not at all."

"Then why don't..."

"I dunno. I didn't think it was that important."

"So… you are wanting to keep your California condo?"

Dave shrugged, "No, I don't guess so, although it's really a cool spot. You can see the ocean from my window. It's about a mile away, but you can still see it. It's got open space, like the living room is huge and opens up to the kitchen…"

He looked over at his passenger and could see the frown lines on her forehead. "But I was gonna talk to a real estate agent some time this week… actually."

She looked over at him questioningly, "Really?"

He chuffed, "Yeah, sure. It's no big deal. That place will get sold in no time flat."

"But what about your things?"

Dave shrugged. "It's just stuff. I can replace it."

Again Evelynn looked at him, confused by his total lackadaisical attitude. They hadn't really discussed homes, or plans for the future. They both just knew they wanted to be together and hoped that the chips would fall in all the right places.

"What? Why are you looking at me like that?" He looked at her from the corner of his eye.

It was Evelynn's turn to shrug. "I don't know, I just thought… I don't think I could just… walk away like that. I couldn't pass those responsibilities off to someone else."

"It's no big deal, really."

"It kinda is. You have utilities that you are still paying for. Mortgage. Who knows what's happened to the food you left in the fridge when you were only planning on staying a couple weeks..."

Dave's brows came together as he thought about the food situation and the left over pizza he left out on the counter, still in its box.

"Your car is still at the airport parking garage..." Evelynn continued.

"Oh, nope, it's not. It was towed finally, didn't I tell you?" he laughed.

Evelynn was having a hard time dismissing his nonchalance. "It's been towed?"

"Yeah, at least we know it's in a safe place."

Evelynn blinked and shook her head, not knowing how to process this information and these new character traits she had discovered. She decided that she had no words and was it really her place to tell him what to do with his old life? But then her thoughts chided, is he going to bring those behaviors into his new life? Would she be able to release control enough to find compromise or are they already doomed before they begin?

After a few moments of silence, Dave reached across the center console and took her hand in his. "Hey, I'll take care of it. All of it. I promise, okay?"

She looked over at him, certain that he could see the worry on her face. She nodded in response, but was still lost in her thoughts.

Dave pulled into the Stanton State Park and a huge grin spread across his face.

She looked over at him from the corner of her eye and couldn't help but giggle at his big cheesy grin.

He drove the rental car past the picnic area, past the camping area and past the playground area down to a smaller side road that followed the river. At the end of the road was the boat dock.

A long, metal pier jutted out into the wide river and boats of many sizes were moored to either side of it. Dave parked the car and went to the trunk to pull out an actual picnic basket.

He scooted around to her car door before she could open it herself and held out his hand to her.

Evelynn giggled. "We're at the river?"

He bit his bottom lip, "I know! Isn't it great?"

He closed the door behind her as she stood to stretch. He took the container of her homemade cookies and put them inside the basket.

"This was your special place? It's the river."

He looked almost hurt, "Well, yeah. I've only really been here a couple times, and I found this little spot by the water... but... we could go someplace else if you want to."

Evelynn put her hands on either side of his face. "No. I love it here. I didn't realize you'd been here at all, much less fell in love with it. I'm glad you love it here." She kissed him on the nose and then his lips. She held out her hand for him to take. "Show me."

They walked down a small hill from the parking lot toward the pier and Dave stopped. He held Evelynn's hand on one side and carried the basket on the other. He pointed down the long pier with the picnic basket and said, "I'm gonna get me one of those babies..."

"You want a boat?"

"Yeah, all the guys say that if you're gonna live here, you'll need a boat. They all have one, and I know Nick is thinking about buying one. We even talked about going in halvesies."

Evelynn couldn't help but smile as he talked about his big plans. Future plans. In small town America... with her.

"I'm gonna put her right there. It's called a slip. That's the slip I want."

She smiled and nodded, trying not to worry, but instead allowed herself to get lost in his excitement. It was a beautiful day, they were spending the afternoon together and he'd planned a picnic lunch for them in his happy place. How could she not love this man?

He was munching on her cookies and she watched him. His brown hair was almost in his eyes and when he wore a cap it would tuft out from under it around his ears and was just long enough now, where it formed curls in the back. He was leaning over the picnic table and had cookie crumbs on his shirt and on his plate in front of him. He licked his finger and used it to adhere the crumbs long enough to get them to his mouth.

This is the man I'm going to spend the rest of my life with, she thought to herself and laughed.

"These cookies are so good." He said when he caught her looking. "I can't stop eating them!"

She smiled and responded, "I'm glad you like them." She looked around at their perfect little picnic nook. A small pavilion was further down, as well as a restroom, water fountain and a small playground. The pavilion had four tables and a barbeque grill available for use.

But Evelynn was more than happy with the table Dave chose. It was perfectly situated a few feet from the river under large old oak trees that shaded them from the summer sun.

She reached out her hand across the table for his. "Thank you for this," she said sincerely.

"Who knew? At the grocery store, they'll prepare an entire lunch for as many people as you tell them! I even bought the cool picnic basket." He paused a moment and ran his thumb across the back of her hand, "I hope we can fill it up and do this again?"

Evelynn nodded happily. "I had all but forgotten what it felt like to leave the Centre and enjoy just sitting still in nature. It really is a special place. Thank you for sharing it with me."

Dave beamed under her praise, but shrugged off the compliment like it was no big deal, "What can I say, I love ya."

Evelynn's smile sparkled all the way up to her eyes. "I love you too."

Chapter Four

Dave came into the kitchen through the sliding glass door from barbequing hamburgers on the deck. He threw his arm around Evelynn's neck and kissed her on the cheek before making his way to the living room. He flopped down on the couch and crossed his ankle on his knee and reached for the television remote.

Evelynn closed her eye as the cacophony of station after station filled the small house. Dave flipped through the channels landing on one for a few moments before moving on to the next.

The television probably had dust on it before Dave started coming over, seeing how little she used it. The busy, static noise was uncomfortable for her. She was used to music, or even silence.

She tried to focus on the work in front of her; slicing tomatoes.

"They're here!" Dave shouted to her. He was looking over his shoulder out the front window's curtains. He stood up to go open the front door.

"Could you please turn off the television?" Evelynn asked.

"Oh, yeah, sure." Dave spun back around, picked up the remote, clicked the button and tossed it back onto the couch.

Evelynn took in a deep breath and released it slowly, knowing that she would go and retrieve the remote later to put it back on the end table.

Dave opened the door and hugged Gwen and shook hands with Nick.

"S'up, brother?"

Gwen brought a covered dish over to the counter where Evelynn was creating the perfect relish tray.

"Where's Erin?" Evelynn asked, as Gwen and Nick came into her home. It was Evelynn and Dave's turn to host their weekly get together.

Ever since the two women of the Bakersfield Fine Arts Centre have found love, they realized how important it was to keep their relationships thriving. So they both vowed to take more time away from the theatre, even if it meant delegating some of their jobs to other staff members. But where they thought they were happy before, their levels of happiness have reached a whole new high.

"We just dropped her off at Gillian's. She has a new foster child that, it just so happens, will be in Erin's class at school in a few weeks, so they are having a play date."

"Is that why Gillian didn't come tonight?" Nick asked. "I feel guilty dumping the girl in her lap."

"No, she barely leaves the farm during the summer. The kids and cows take up most of her time."

"Aren't she and Tom getting married soon?"

"Ding! Time?" Evelynn laughed as she raised her arms up over her head.

"Exactly twelve minutes." Dave checked the microwave clock.

Gwen and Nick looked at each other and then back at Evelynn.

"We were wondering how long it would take before someone mentioned a wedding." Dave and Evelynn high-fived each other.

"I think I win," Dave said. "I guessed ten minutes."

Evelynn nodded, "Yeah, I gave us the benefit of the doubt, I said thirty."

Gwen and Nick laughed. "Wait," Gwen added. "We didn't mention *your* wedding, does that still count?"

"'Fraid it does," Dave retorted.

"Lots of wedding fever happening in Bakersfield lately."

Nick leaned over and kissed his girlfriend, anxious for the day he can put a ring on her finger. "Yep, I guess you're right," he laughed. "I just can't get this one to say 'yes'!"

Gwen gently elbowed him in the stomach. "You know the answer is 'yes', but you haven't asked. I don't see a ring… Plus, we have to wait our turn. The theatre is booked through December."

"Spring then."

"You… have got a date." Gwen stretched up on her toes to be nose to nose with Nick and kissed him. A quick little peck. And then just once more.

"You heard her folks. You're my witnesses!"

"Can we get through *Annie Get Your Gun* first? It's our season opener and I need your bride on her toes since I will be doing double duty."

"Ding! Time?" Gwen called out and could barely keep from laughing.

"What? What did you guys bet on?"

Nick checked his watch. "Theatre talk. And the answer is: fourteen minutes and twenty-two seconds."

Gwen was holding on the counter bending over with laughter. We were just talking about that on the way over here."

"Okay, that's it. No more wedding or work talk. Agreed?" Evelynn proposed.

"Agreed." Gwen nodded.

The boys nodded too. "Let's eat!" Dave said as he picked up the tray of burger toppings the girls were working on. "Those burgers are grilled to perfection!"

He led the way to the back deck while the others followed.

After dinner, Gwen helped Evelynn load the dishwasher. Before closing it up and turning it on, Evelynn scanned the counter, the sink and the table for any remaining dishes. And just for good measure, she leaned over and looked out the back door.

Gwen could hear the audible sigh as she slid open the door, walked out to the patio table, picked up Dave's dishes and marched back inside.

"I was gonna get that, babe."

Evelynn closed the door with her elbow and gave Gwen an exasperated look.

Gwen didn't even have to comment; she knew what was bothering her perfectly organized best friend. She tried to keep her smirking to a minimum.

Evelynn heavy-handed the dishwasher adding in the last few pieces before pushing the 'start' button triumphantly.

It wasn't even a full moment later that Dave came walking into the kitchen carrying tongs. "Here ya go, I brought these in for you. They were on the grill. Guess you missed them, huh." He smiled at her and went back outside completely oblivious to her mood.

Evelynn opened her mouth to speak but just looked at Gwen with the tongs in her hand...

Gwen bit her bottom lip to hold back a snicker. "Nick is sentimental."

Evelynn paused, furrowing her brow and gave her that, what-does-that-have-to-do-with-anything look.

"We've been trying to clean out his parent's house and he just... can't let anything go."

"Ahhh," Evelynn nodded in understanding. Her very best friend was a minimalist. She had no need for "extra" things.

"His mom saved every one of their art projects and reports from their school years. Four boys-worth of memories in boxes." She paused for emphasis. "And he can't let any of them go."

Evelynn laughed.

"His ball caps? You'll never in a million years guess how many he has. It became his 'thing' for the television show, right? So, everyone would give him one for each and every episode. And he wants to keep them *all*."

"Guess you'll need a separate room for just hats." Evelynn couldn't help but giggle at her pain.

Gwen stared at her blankly, "There *is* a room of just hats."

At that moment the boys came in from the back yard, laughing and carrying on until they saw their women's faces.

They looked at each other and then back at the girls. "Are we in trouble?" Nick asked.

Immediately their faces softened when they both realized that despite their imperfections, they were both pretty lucky this second time around.

"We thought you might be ready to play cards, but if you wanna wait, we can go watch the tube."

"No, I'm ready." Evelynn quickly answered.

"Me too." Gwen echoed.

Nick leaned over and whispered, "They hate the television..."

Dave stared blankly as if all the questions of the universe had just been answered for him. "That explains a lot."

Gwen went over to the kitchen table and scooped up a dozen or so brochures. She flipped through them briefly, "You guys getting a boat?"

Evelynn jerked her head toward Dave.

"Yes, ma'am!" He strutted his way over to take the stack from her. "This one is the top choice and this is the runner up." He put them in order and showed them to Gwen.

"These are nice. Are you taking up fishing?"

"Isn't that kind of a rule around here?" he laughed. "What else is there to do in this little bitty town?" He nudged his best friend, "Am I right?"

Nick rolled his eyes apologetically. "He just lets the words roll right out of his mouth," Nick said shaking his head. Nick came over and took one from the pile and handed it to Gwen to put on top. He stepped back and winked moving his index finger between himself and her.

"You too?" It was Gwen's turn to roll her eyes.

"Guilty."

"It would be a nice getaway. Picnics along the river; you girls could sit and read on the deck while floating down the river?" Nick hugged Gwen from behind, rocking them back and forth painting the picture for her.

"Boys and their toys."

"Yes, but..."Evelynn attempted a rebuttal.

Nick clapped and rubbed the palms of his hands together. "Welp! Who's ready for some cards?"

The dark brown banner with big yellow letters announced the Bakersfield Fine Arts Centre's Open House! The lobby was decorated with fall leaves and shimmering pumpkins, and gourds. The burning candles gave not only a warm and welcoming glow, but added the scent of fall.

Tables were lined up along the edges of the room and a few spilled into the auditorium. The teachers meandered about answering questions and giving tours of the facility. Returning children proudly showed their friends where the classrooms were and even demonstrated a few "moves" they'd learned last year.

Evelynn and Gwen looked absolutely ravishing in their fall floor length maxi dresses. Evelynn had her dark hair swept up into a French roll and Gwen wore her long blond hair down her back.

Dave wandered around the room with his camera on his shoulder capturing the excitement for the local news channel and also for their website. He walked around the room being careful not to interfere. He slipped over beside his bride to be and leaned in to plant a kiss on her cheek. She anticipated it and without interrupting her conversation with a parent, stuck her cheek out for easy access. She smiled as he walked on doing his thing.

When the event finally came to a close and all the instructors slipped off their heels and let down their hair, Gwen announced the results.

"Forty-two brand new students!" The room cheered. "That's a record for us!" She looked down at her papers and flipped through, "Hang on, I won't bore you with all the details, but I wanted to share a couple more stats with you. We had twelve kids sign up because of the summer camps. So, great job everyone. And we have..." she ran her finger down the page, "A ninety-two percent return rate!" She threw her arms in the air and the room applauded. "We must be doing something right!"

"And, to celebrate..." Evelynn interjected, "Bring it out, honey."

Dave wheeled a cart into the room that carried bottles of champagne and champagne glasses.

All the women in the room cheered and Gwen added, "No champagne for you, Miss Danni, there's sparkling cider for our minors!"

Danni rolled her eyes and laughed.

Everyone filled a glass and gathered in somewhat of a circle in the center of the lobby. Evelynn raised her glass, "Here's to you, the amazing teachers that make this place so great." They clinked and sipped.

Gillian spoke up next, "And here's to you, our fearless leaders. Your tireless efforts may never really be recognized by the public, but we here see behind the scenes. You sacrifice your time and energy and put your heart and soul into this place, and it shows. Without you, none of this would be here. Cheers!"

Evelynn and Gwen shoulder-hugged each other and tried desperately not to cry and ruin their make-up.

"Now you, Miss Gwen!" Jenni shouted.

Gwen smiled and gently dabbed under her eyes with her index finger. She thought for a moment, "Here's to another memory-making season at the Centre. One that will be filled with life changes and love changes and great friends creating great things." The glasses clinked but it soon turned into a giant group hug.

Dave leaned back against the wall, smiling and filming everything.

"Speaking of life changes and love changes, how are the wedding plans coming?"

Evelynn breathed out and rolled her eyes. "There is so much to do!" she laughed. "I don't remember there being so much!"

We only had the classes back then, remember?" Gwen reminded her. "And now your work load has tripled."

"That's true," she laughed.

"Is there anything you need us to do?" Gillian asked.

Evelynn waved the comment away, "Shooooot, we still have three whole months! That's more than enough time for theatre people!"

The group of women nodded and laughed.

"Last time, we were gluing beads on her wedding dress the night before." Gwen snickered.

"True   story."   Evelynn   nodded   in confirmation.

The teachers all stayed and helped put the lobby back to its original state and got everything cleaned up before it was just Evelynn and Dave walking through the building turning off all the lights.

"You amaze me," he whispered as he pulled her into his embrace.

She smiled and fell in comfortably to his back and forth sway. "Thank you."

"And your staff really seems to love you."

Evelynn looked around at nothing as a smile crossed her face, "And I love them too. Such a good group of women. Gwen and I are really lucky. Not all the drama and back-biting that usually goes on."

They danced in silence a moment more, before Dave could feel Evelynn take in a deep breath and let it out.

He pulled back to look at her face. "Babe, tears? Are you alright?"

She nodded. "I guess I'm just a bit overwhelmed at the moment. I don't want anything to fall through the cracks. I have so much on my plate right now."

Dave stepped back and took her hands in his. "But what about all that... you said..."

"Oh honey, that's all theatre talk. I don't want them to have to worry. No one, other than Gwen really understands how much time it takes to get ... even... tonight's open house put together. I now have classes to teach, one full-length musical to produce, a holiday dance recital…"her gaze went off to the left, "I need to talk to Gwen and Jeanne to see if they want a holiday art show…" she turned and looked directly into Dave's eye, "…and… the most spectacular wedding anyone has ever seen, to plan." She smiled and leaned in to kiss her fiancée.

He pulled her close to him and she wrapped her arms around his neck. "Let me help you."

"You have enough on your own plate. You have to settle your stuff in California, find a job, and we need to start looking for a house."

"That can wait, if you want."

"Honey, I don't mind. You said you are uncomfortable living in the same house that my ex and I lived in and I totally get that. I'm good with moving into a place that will be just ours."

He kissed her again, "Mmmm," he breathed, "We'd better get out of here before I take advantage of your intoxicated state." He kissed her neck and brought kisses up to her lips.

She giggled and squirmed in response.

"Come on," he stepped back and swung her hands in his, "you were a good girl today, let me treat you with some ice-cream."

"I knew I loved you for a reason!"

Gwen tapped on the open door of Evelynn's office.   Evelynn looked up from her desk and smiled at the intrusion.

"You busy?"

"Always, but never too busy for you. Come on in. How are you *not* busy?" Evelynn laughed.

"I am. I was just in one of those phases that I'm staring off into space, and to the outsider it would *look* like I was getting nothing done."

Evelynn nodded in understanding. "I know those."

"So, I decided to come down here and *look* busy instead." Gwen laughed.

"Nice. So essentially, you're keeping both of us from accomplishing anything productive." Evelynn cocked her eyebrow.

Gwen pretended to be in deep thought and answered, "Yeah, basically."

"Great plan. I like it." Evelynn laid her pen down and pushed her notebook to the side. "So, what were you thinking on so heavily?"

"You, mainly." Gwen answered honestly. "There I was hemming and hawing about whether to fall in love with Nick for months and I almost ruined everything, and here you are, you meet this guy and now in only a few months you're going to be his wife. It's hard to wrap my head around it. Are you sure he's the one? I mean... it hasn't been that long? How do you know?"

Evelynn shrugged, but a smile spread across her face. "I'll be honest, I do get nervous thinking about what I'm about to do. And if it were you, I'd probably caution you against it. But, it feels right. When I'm with him, I can't think of any place else I'd rather be." Evelynn smiled. "Lame answer, right? You were probably hoping for a little more scientific?"

Gwen shrugged. "I don't know what I was hoping for. Just... that you *had* an answer, maybe? That you have at least thought about it? Not just... you know, diving in, just because..."

Evelynn laughed, "And why are you asking me? You're going through the same thing! How do you know that Nick is the one?"

Gwen shrugged, "I *don't* know. It still worries me that he's going to wake up and wonder what he's doing with me."

"Why would you think that? He loves you! And you guys are perfect together."

Gwen couldn't hold back the smile. "I know. We are perfect together. And he loves Erin. Although, I might have scared him too much. I mean, yes, we're together, but I may have scared the marriage right out of him."

Evelynn smiled calmly, "For the millionth time, he wants to marry you. He would have married you ten times over by now, but you just... wouldn't trust. You guys will be married. Now it's his turn to choose."

"But you and Dave seem so different. I really thought you would have gotten bored, or... too irritated with him by now."

Evelynn leaned back in her chair and her face reflected her heart. "Oh no. I have only wanted to run the other direction once... maybe twice. That time he got a speeding ticket and he blamed everyone else and carried on for hours yelling at everyone and everything, as if we pushed his foot down." Gwen nodded, remembering that day. Evelynn continued, "We're so different..." Evelynn laughed, "and yet so much a like. In the core of our relationship, we are dead on. We both believe the same things. We want the same things for our futures. We like and even dislike so many of the same things. It's like we made a check-list and there are more checks in the FOR column than there are in the AGAINST column. We really are well matched."

"I would have never picked him for you." Gwen giggled.

Evelynn laughed easily with her friend. "I know. I wouldn't have either. But, in addition to the black and white stuff, he spoke directly to my heart. He just seemed to move right in. Like there was a space and he filled it perfectly." She leaned forward on her desk and propped her head on her left hand. "You know about that space. We talked about it.. We were both feeling that... that... emptiness. And we both tried to fill it with work."

Gwen nodded, acknowledging everything Evelynn was saying. "But along came Erin..."

"Exactly. You just knew. And you were so busy celebrating in the perfectness of being a mother, that you didn't even notice that God wasn't finished blessing you. He doesn't want you to do it all alone. And I believe He has the same thoughts for me. Maybe not being a parent, but... Dave is definitely my helpmeet. He supports me and respects me and wants to see me achieve, all while he is standing beside me. I've never felt that before.   He isn't competing with me, he... is cheering for me."

"Yes, that I can see." Gwen leaned back and crossed her ankles on the corner of Evelynn's desk, "But... how... can you..."

"Faith.   Faith, Guinevere.   I have faith in God's plan for me. I have faith in the feeling that I feel when I am with him. If we constantly need something tangible in everything, then why do we need faith? I have faith in this man. I have faith in our future together. Yes, it's going to take some adjusting... " she paused and closed her eyes for a second, mentally counting off all the little irritants that she will have to make way for, but then continued, "...but I really and truly believe that we were meant to be together."

"I wish I saw things like that. So clearly."

"You do. You just don't give yourself the credit. You don't trust yourself enough to know when God is whispering to you."

"That's the truth. But I'm getting better."

"You are. Do you want me to have Dave whisper to Nick about a double wedding?" Evelynn bounced her eyebrows.

Gwen laughed, and dropped her feet back to the floor. "No," she blushed. "This is your time. I still have to work on my 'faith' and then I will get to celebrate with as much assuredness as you and your husband to be." Gwen stood up and walked around the desk to embrace her best friend. "I'm glad you are so happy. I wouldn't want to see you any other way, ever again."

"I am happy. And I am even happier that we can share in this phase of life too."

"Yeah, okay... On that note, I'm going back to my office to actually do some work before I start to cry."

"At least they'd be happy tears."

"Yep, got no time for that. I'm gone..." but she winked before she rounded the corner.

Chapter Five

Evelynn and Gwen stood behind Betty as they all hovered around the computer on the corner of Betty's desk. They had just installed a new software to help keep track of the students, payments and even ticket sales. Betty shook her head, and lifted her glasses and set them on top of her head.

"That saying about old dogs and new tricks, I'm starting to believe it!" she rubbed her eyes.

"It's a learning curve for all of us, but if we can get the hang of it..."

"I'm out of a job!" Betty squawked.

"Not gonna happen." Gwen squeezed her shoulders and looked back down to the step by step pamphlet.

"Okay, it says to enter the student name in Field Seven," Gwen was reading.

"Is that the student or the parent of the student."

"Oh, good question," Evelynn said. "I don't know if it can be adjusted to students who are minors."

"Hang on, let me find it..."Gwen traced her finger along the folded pages.

It was then that the main door flew open and slammed against the back wall.

"Whoohooo!" a voice called out.

Before the ladies could respond a male figured poured himself into the room. "I am here!" he said, his voice filling up the small office.

The three women looked at each other and then back at him. He easily stood over six feet tall. His arms were above his head while making his entrance. His light brown skin was a sharp contrast to the cream-colored fur coat he wore. The collar was pulled up so it framed his face. His hair was cropped short and close but had a design shaved into the sides where it met his perfectly shaped silhouette of a beard. His sunglasses had a diamond rim and covered half his face. His stomach pushed through the coat's opening and his slacks tapered down tight to his ankles, leaving his size thirteen, expensive leather shoes sticking out at the bottom acting as a stand. And if you were able to catch a glimpse at just the right time, you would see that his socks were rainbow colored with white stars.

The girls were speechless. But Betty, being the office manager and polite to a fault, spoke first. "Can we help you?"

He disassembled his pose and looked at the tiny people hunkered behind a desk. His upper lip curled up. "Oh no, honey. I am here to help you."

No one knew what to say. His entire countenance filled the room and suffocated all trains of thought.

"Alright then," Betty continued, "How can we help you help us."

He pulled a piece of paper from his coat pocket and read from it. "I'm supposed to be meeting someone named Evie St. Lawrence. Oh, girl, that's a great name. I hope that's her stage name, 'cause that's cute."

Evelynn stepped to the side, "I'm Evelynn."

He tipped his sunglasses forward to get a better look. "I'd go with Evie, if I was you, but that's just me."

Evelynn looked questioningly at Gwen and tried not to laugh, and saw that Gwen was struggling too.

"So, I am here to coordinate your wedding, honey. It's gonna be beautiful, it's gonna be gorgeous... you're going to look amazing because I am amazing."

"Wait... what?"

"You're a wedding coordinator?" Gwen asked.

"Baby, I can be anything you want me to be, but this week I'm here in this lil town that even Jesus himself is trying to avoid because that lil man of yours," he pointed to Evelynn, "told me that you needed my help. And baby, I just can't turn down a man in need; ...his lil pouty, squishy face."

"You... know Dave?" Evelynn asked still trying to sort things out in her mind.

"Girl yes, me and the lil man go way back. I used to be a make-up artist and when I added wedding coordinator to my resume, he helped me out by shooting some commercials for me. I'm just doin' him a solid."

"You are from California?" Betty asked.

He locked eyes with her and cocked his eyebrow. He swept his hand from the top of his head and down his body, as if to say, *Isn't it obvious?*

Betty nodded, "Oh, yes, I see..." She dropped her gaze and gave a sideways glance at the other two, not exactly sure how to proceed.

"It was very sweet of you to come all this way," Gwen offered.

"Oh girl, don't I know it." He pulled a small vial from his coat pocket and tilted his head back pushing his sunglasses up. He proceeded to squeeze the bottle just enough until one drop of liquid fell into his eye. He did the same with the other. He pinched his eyes shut, shook his head and popped his head so his glasses would fall back into place.

"Um... what... is your name, please?"

"Lucas Lesley Powers. My momma knew what she was gettin. Ain't no surprises here, no ma'am." He ran a finger across his perfectly shaped eyebrows.

"Well, thank you for coming," Evelynn smiled and walked toward him extending her hand.

He shook it, "The pleasure's all mine. But now that we got the formalities out the way, I need to go find my room, and honey, I could use a drink like nobody's business. Where's the closest liquor store? Oh never mind, I can find one. Okay honeys, you be good and don't you worry, Lucas has got it all under control." He turned to make his exit but reentered the room once again. "Oh, and hair and make-up, tomorrow. Noon for you." And he flitted, literally, out the door.

The office was silent for a few moments.

Gwen furrowed her brow. "Dave got you a wedding coordinator?"

Evelynn had her hands on both sides of her face and when she turned to Gwen there was a sheen in her eyes. She nodded her head, "He got me a wedding coordinator... Isn't that sweet?" A tear slipped from her eye and bobbed along her fingertips until it could find passage down the side of her hand.

Gwen giggled, "It is sweet... I just can't seem to picture those two as friends. He's quite a character."

Evelynn nodded, her brow wrinkling in concern.

"Maybe he will be just what the doctor ordered." Betty optimistically offered.

"Whoa, where are you?" Gwen asked when she walked into Evelynn's office.

Evelynn turned away from her open French doors and looked nonchalantly at her best friend. "I'm here. Just thinking. What a day."

"That's not a starry eyed look... but it's not a planning, or choreographing look either... so, what's up?"

She shrugged. "Nothing, honestly."

Gwen raised her eyebrows and flopped down on the chaise crossing her ankles, "But..."

Another shrug. "I'm just..."

"Dave..."

"Yes." Evelynn smiled coyly. "I guess I'm anxious to see how God is going to work all this out."

Gwen furrowed her brow, encouraging Evelynn to continue with her train of thought.

"I know I want to marry him. I know that. No doubts there, but sometimes our little differences are enough to make me think about throwing in the towel... or strangling him... or strangling him *with* the towel... and then he sends me a wedding planner."

Gwen laughed. "I think that comes with all relationships, doesn't it? I mean," she bobbed her shoulder, "that was one of the many reasons I kept putting space between Nick and me was because I couldn't face all of the changes I would have to make to fit him into my life and let go of all the damage Mark did."

Evelynn nodded. "I've been alone for a while now and yet it seems like yesterday that Carlos was in my house."

"It might have been yesterday. He is kinda shady like that."

Evelynn laughed, "Don't say that! You put it out into the universe!"

"So, do you think you're rushing into things?"

"No." Evelynn looked down at her nails and absent-mindedly pushed back the cuticle on her pinky, before looking back up at Gwen. "Do... do you?"

Gwen furrowed her brows. "I... I don't know. That's not really something I can answer. To me, it feels like you're going too fast, but what do I know? Dating when you're older has a completely different set of rules. And I like that. You don't have to hint at things and hope he figures things out. You can just... talk. I love that. If we have a problem, we can discuss it. But, I had to almost completely lose everything before I realized this new dating behavior." Gwen rolled her eyes. "Oh, I was so stupid. And now, I've probably scared *him* so bad that he's going to make *me* wait for years before he marries me." Gwen nervously laughed.

Evelynn laughed with her, "No, I'm sure that's not going to happen. He loves you so much. I think he wants to make sure that you're comfortable. No doubts."

"Will there ever be a day like that? I love him, I know that, but I still have doubts as to whether we're going to make it. 'Cause, seriously... I'm not doing this again!" she laughed, breaking the tension.

Evelynn laughed easily, "Same!"

"So... you have doubts?"

"Yes? Well... no? It's not that. I think I just have to find patience and learn to accept him for the way that he *actually* is, not who I think he *should* be. Does that make sense?" Evelynn looked off in the distance recalling a memory, "Here's an example of ... my... let's call it a dilemma." She paused, smiling as she shook her head. "So he was coming over for dinner and I was rushing, because

I had...oh, it was the day that we repainted Studio A, remember?"   Gwen nodded and Evelynn continued. "Okay, so I rushed home, showered and got started on dinner. I'm standing at the counter making our salad and he comes in the front door and stops short when he sees me." She paused taking in a breath, "He says, 'Oh, I didn't know we were goin' all casual tonight.'

Gwen gasped and opened her mouth, obviously feeling the underlying insult.

"Yeah! Exactly. Sure, my hair was in a messy bun and I was wearing my glasses. And... okay, so I was wearing a sweatshirt and my yoga pants. But it's not like he was wearing a tie or anything! So, I apologized, explaining that I just barely made it home."

"What'd he say?"

"He said, 'It's okay. You look cute."

"Awww."

Evelynn blushed.   "Yeah but wait..." she giggled. "So he grabs a carrot off the counter and started eating it... chewing with his mouth open..." she looked up at the ceiling in exasperation and shook her head. "So I came out from behind the counter to put the salad on the table and I hear him choking on the carrot!" She started laughing.

Gwen was confused at how to respond.

"He was choking on the carrot because..." she laughed again, "...because... he saw me in my yoga pants and said... I'll leave out the curse words, he said, 'You look hot in those pants!'"

Evelynn and Gwen burst out in laughter as Evelynn turned several shades of crimson.

"See? What am I supposed to do with that?" she went on, "so for every irritant, he comes back with something so... adorable, I don't even know what to do with him."

"Well, didn't you say this was his first real relationship?"

"Yeah, pretty much. But it's not mine, so... I expect him to behave a certain way and he... he chokes on a carrot."

"But even with his... quirkiness, isn't it nice not to have to be on guard? He is who he is. What you see is what you get. And you never have to feel on the defensive when you're with him. I remember that Carlos would constantly question and doubt you," Gwen offered.

Evelynn frowned at the memory. "Even now, I just assume Dave's going to ask me about how I spent money or time and I catch myself having answers prepared for him. So, yeah, I love that he is so... real." She paused, "I guess we both have to figure out how to fit with one another. I do love him. Not the kind of giggly love, but a solid... secure kind of love."

"Don't you miss that fluttery feeling?"

Evelynn thought about it for a moment. "No, I don't think so. I like this certainty. And if I have to trade the butterfly feeling to have someone faithful and honest and that's willing to go through the learning curve with me, then it is a trade I am happy to make."

"Well said. But... I still get butterflies when Nick kisses me. Oh, that man... "

"Yeah, sure, but I have Lucas Lesley Powers."

The two girls giggled, happy for the other and happy for their own lot in love.

Evelynn walked out of her office into the main office and watched Betty's, Gillian's and Gwen's eyes widen into artificial smiles of horror.

"Tada!" Lucas snapped his fingers and held out his hands to showcase his work.

Evelynn took a few steps forward and silently took in a deep breath and exhaled. There were no words spoken from anyone. Just staring.

Lucas produced a can of aerosol hairspray and doused Evelynn's already concreted style in a cloud of stickiness, while waving it from his own face.

Evelynn's hair was teased and rolled to four times its usual size. She wore a mint colored, high-waisted robe with buttons. There was pink tissue paper tucked between the collar and her face...

Finally Gwen looked at the other women and then to her best friend and asked her, "Have *you* seen it?"

Evelynn slowly blinked and nodded.

Betty stepped forward, "You look so different."

"I know!" Lucas squealed. "Isn't make-up amazing?"

"It is." Gillian finally commented. "We need someone like you on our make-up staff for our productions. This blending is flawless."

"Oh girl, stop..." Lucas feigned humility and brushed her comment away with a swat of his hand.

"That's a lot of make-up."

Evelynn nodded, "I don't think I've worn make-up this thick since I was the wicked witch of the West."

"I could probably write my name in your cheek."

Lucas huffed, "Uh, layering... "

Evelynn looked to her best friend for some honest feedback. She lifted her one eyebrow, with a great deal of effort, in question.

Gwen stepped forward. "You look like... a combination of Beyonce and Tammy Wynette in drag."

Lucas jumped up and down and clapped his hands in quick succession in front of his face. "Oh honey," he placed his hands to his face as if he had just won the Miss America crown. "I know, isn't she fabulous?"

Gwen looked up at the six foot two man and back down to her five foot eleven friend and couldn't help but smile. "I... I..." she nodded her head smiling, "... am speechless."

Evelynn stifled a laugh herself, and tightened her lips so as not to smile and crack her foundation.

"Lucas, I think she may be *too* fabulous for the humble little wedding that she's planning."

"Omagawd, I know." Lucas leaned forward and tapped Gwen's forearm. "But don't you worry about that. I can take care of that lil problem. Don't you worry, Lucas is here." He turned and made his way back to Evelynn's office and the women stood in silence.

"I can barely lift my eyelids," Evelynn finally said.

"It really is beautiful work." Gillian came closer to "inspect" her face. "Flawless, but..."

"It's not our Evie," Betty stated the obvious.

Lucas emerged from the back room carrying his tools of the trade and rubbing his left temple. "I have got to run, and take care of this hangover. I need something on my stomach, Lawd."

"Hangover?" Betty questioned.

"Yes, girl."

All the women covered their mouths and giggled. "It was your first night." Gwen said through her laughter.

He shrugged and felt it should be self-explanatory. "Where can I go to find some good Southern cookin'?"

Evelynn spoke up, "Try Adam's Rib. They have amazing barbeque."

"I hear you. I'm gone."

When they heard the door click shut the laughter could no longer be contained.

"Bakersfield will never be the same," Gwen giggled.

"I am never going to be the same!" Evelynn pointed at her face.

"I know I don't have much of a say in this matter," Betty started, "...but please, don't wear your hair and make-up like that. It's just not natural."

"Don't worry, I have no intention of wearing it like this. I don't know how I'm going to tell him..."

"I know, he was so proud!" Gillian sympathized.

Evelynn shrugged. "I have to go shower and get this off me."

"Want me to stay and help brush your hair out?" Gwen offered.

"No, I'll be okay. Don't you have to go to the post office?

"I do. And a couple other places, but I'll be back in a few hours so we can work on our classes."

"We're gonna take off too, then," Gillian added. "Mom and I have to get some back-to-school shopping done. But I'll be back in town again next Tuesday, and I'll bring in my class outlines."

"Sounds good."

Evelynn heard the door to the Centre open and click closed, but she paid no attention. She was in the main dance room with only half the lights on, giving the room a soft, almost romantic feel. She was choreographing for an upcoming class. She swayed back and forth and waited for the music to tell her what to do. When she found a section of movements she liked, she would pause and write them down so she could teach them later.

She was busy doing just that, when a body slid up behind her and ran his fingers down both her arms. She took in a deep breath recognizing his unique cologne. She closed her eyes and allowed him to lead her back into the center of the room. She could feel his breath on her neck. He wrapped one hand around her waist while holding her other hand in his. He pressed her close to his body, so she could follow his movements.

He danced her around the room in this position for a while before he spun her away from him and pulling her back in against him. Her face was only inches from his.

"Carlos..."

He smiled at her and continued moving her body where he wanted it to go and making her look and feel beautiful in the dimly lit room. His hands never left her but made themselves at home on her perfect dancer's figure.

They twisted and turned and he guided her beautifully feeling the rhythm of the music. When the song finally came to a close, he spun her back to his chest and dipped her backwards, then effortlessly pulling her back up. His lips found hers and he finished the song with a kiss. His hands caressed the back of her head and slid down her back.

Evelynn's heart pounded in her chest and she made herself pull away. She brought her fingers to her lips still warm from his touch, while confusion clouded her thoughts. She took a few steps back hoping to create space between them.

"My Angel," Carlos took a step closer.

"Hey Carlos," Gwen spoke from the doorway. She looked over at her best friend and saw both a look of guilt and thankfulness.

Carlos stared at Evelynn a moment more before turning his attentions to the intruder. "Guinevere, how lovely to see you again." His Latin accent would make anything sound amazing. But Gwen was in protector mode.

"Yeah," she sighed out, "Wish I could believe you."

Evelynn remained silent as she took steps backward away from him. Her whole body and face and movements screamed out shame... guilt... fear? She kept her eyes down and her hand rested at her chest. When she reached the mirrors, she leaned back against them and prayed that she could just disappear. Right now.

"Evelynn, mi vida, I must speak with you," Carlos purred, holding out his hand for her to take.

Gwen stepped in, making an executive decision for her friend. "She can't right now, Carlos. I'm going to have to ask you to leave."

"Please, I made a mistake, tu me perdonarias," Carlos implored her once again, paying no attention to Gwen's words.

Evelynn was frozen, speechless.

Gwen came into the room and stood between the two dancers, "Carlos, please. Please go. It's not a good time." Her voice was gentle as her heart went out to her friend.

Carlos finally looked and acknowledged Gwen and nodded.

"I'm sorry. Another time..." He looked back at his ex-wife once again, and left the room.

Evelynn spoke no words but slid to the floor and cried. Gwen came and sat beside her wrapping her arms around her shoulders. They sat in silence until the sun had set and the tears had run dry.

Gwen didn't bring up Carlos for two whole days. Evelynn was clearly not herself. She hadn't come into the Centre one day, telling Lucas she wasn't feeling well. And the next day she was quiet, reserved and didn't really get any work done. More along the lines of having the best of intentions, but all she could do was sit and stare out the window.

Gwen came into her office to see Evelynn sitting on her chaise. "Are you going to tell me what happened?"

Evelynn looked over at her best friend and looked down again. Gwen could see that her chin was quivering. Evelynn looked up again as a tear slipped down her cheek. "I kissed him."

Gwen's eyebrows went up and she came further into the room and sat in Evelynn's office chair.

"I didn't mean to," she continued, "... it just happened." She went on to tell Gwen the whole story. By the end she was in tears all over again. "I didn't mean for it to happen. But Gwen, all... all of those feelings came back. I wasn't... I didn't... think I'd ever see him again... and..." she broke down.

"Hey, hey..."Gwen scooted over to the chaise. She lifted Evelynn's legs and tucked herself underneath, leaning over to hug her waist. "It's going to be okay..."

"No it's not... what if I have messed everything up?"

"It was just one kiss... I'm sure that..."

Evelynn's eyes dropped to her hands.

Gwen sat back up and looked her in the eye. "It was just one kiss, right?"

Evelynn nodded, "And the dance."

"And the dance... that's all... right?"

Evelynn nodded again, "Except that..."

"Except that... what?"

"He's been texting me."

Gwen scrunched her eyes closed and silently prayed, *Lord, there's a whole lot of cuss words that are wanting to come out of my mouth, please don't let them...* Gwen believed Carlos could sell a popsicle to an Eskimo. He was a liar and a thief and a whole list of other not-nice words.

"Are you answering them? Or ignoring them?" Gwen tried to keep her voice even. She had lived through the aftermath of this man once before and was not happy having to revisit those same emotions.

"I told him that I had moved on. I told him not to text me anymore..."

"And?"

"He tells me how beautiful I am and how much he has missed by not staying with me..." She pulled out her cell phone, which she had tucked between her body and the back of the chaise. She pushed a few buttons unlocking the screen and pulled up her messages. "I am ashamed that I had to go away to realize how amazing you truly are. I never want to be without you again. You are my passion. My angel. Please say you'll see me," she read.

Gwen shook her head, "Man, he's good."

Evelynn raised her eyebrows, "Right?"

"What did you tell him?"

"I told him that I was getting married in five months."

"And he said?"

Evelynn lowered her head and read from her phone again, "Don't do anything, please. I beg you, papi. Give me one more chance. Please meet me. If you can say you do not love me, then I will give you my blessing. But your lips on mine, tell another story." She dropped the phone on her lap and shook her head.

Gwen looked at her, waiting for her to continue, and when she offered no more information she spoke. "You're not entertaining the idea, are you?"

The sheen covered her eyes as she merely shrugged her shoulders.

Gwen shook Evelynn's knees. "Evie! Stop that! You know who this man is! You're about to marry one of the nicest, sweetest, okay, perhaps a little ill-mannered, but honest men, I've ever met. And he loves you.... LOVES you, Evie!"

"I know."

"He's your helpmeet. You said so! You said you knew he was who you were supposed to be with! Faith! Faith, you said!"

"I know."

"So what is happening here?"

"I don't know," Evelynn shrugged. "I can't lie. I still have feelings for him. He left and... there was no 'goodbye', no... closure... no argument... it was like he just disappeared. Got lost on his way home..."

"For two years? Come on, now." Gwen was blunt. "You know he is not good for you."

Evelynn furrowed her brow. "I do know that. I don't know what's wrong with me. Even when we were still together, I couldn't figure out why I was still with him. He just... I don't know, does something to me. He says he loves me. He says he wants another chance. Maybe he's changed? Maybe I owe him that to see..."

Gwen took in a deep breath and pushed it back out. "Evie. I'm going to have to say some hard things, so you just need to bear with me.... That is not love. He doesn't love you. Deep down, I know you know that. He ..."

"Why did he come back then?"

"Who cares! It's not for noble causes I'm quite sure!"

Evelynn shook her head, "But we don't know that... what if he's changed?"

"Okay, let's look at that for a minute. Right now- because we are even HAVING THIS CONVERSATION- you need to call Dave and tell him that the wedding is off. That you were wrong. That your faith in everything you want for your future is wrong. That you don't trust what God has in store for you. Is that about right? Go ahead, make the call."

Evelynn sat up straight and was about to speak when Gwen continued.

"Because if you are even slightly thinking about giving this..." she pursed her lips together to keep her words Christian-like, "... person a moment more of your time, then you do not love Dave. I don't care how confused you may think you feel, or what you think you owe that man, but if you go to see him, you do not love Dave, end of story. Because if you did, Carlos wouldn't even be able to tempt you."

Evelynn took the tongue lashing as tears slipped from her eyes.

"And I know you DO love Dave," she continued, her voice softening, "because I saw you that day; the day of the dance. I saw that look on your face."

Evelynn nodded.

"You don't *owe* Carlos one more moment of your time." Gwen took Evelynn's hand into her own. "He doesn't love you, honey. Tell me you can see that. I've said it over and over again. Actions speak louder than words. If he says one thing but does another, always follow the actions. That's where you'll find the truth. Do his actions say 'love' to you? His words are amazing. They always have been. But the truth has been there all along, we just didn't want to see it."

Evelynn nodded again.

"I love you. Dave loves you. He might be a dork, but he's your dork. He may not be all fire and pass-si-oon," she butchered the Spanish accent, "but he proves to you over and over again that his love is real."

Gwen pulled Evie's hand to her lips and kissed the back of it. They sat in silence for a few moments. Gwen reached across Evelynn's legs to the corner of her desk where a box of tissue set. She grabbed it and handed it to Evelynn taking a couple for herself first.

Evelynn dried her tears and blew her nose. "Thank you. I needed to hear that."

Gwen smiled. "You're welcome. Don't make me do it again.

"I love you, Guinevere Collins."

"I love you, Evie St. Lawrence, soon to be Ripke." Gwen rolled her eyes. "What a trade-off" she laughed. "Maybe he should take your name!"

They both laughed.

Chapter Six

Lucas walked into the auditorium holding his hand to his forehead. He wore his sunglasses and was sporting the "tattered look". His shirt fit snuggly, making him look like he was about "four months along" and had faux tears and he complimented it with jeans and alligator skin shoes.

Gwen and Evelynn watched him navigate the chairs in the aisles.

"What do you do all night?" Gwen frowned at him wondering how he could look so tore up every single morning.

Lucas raised his eyebrows and held out his hand, "Girl..." he looked away and shook his head... "Just... no. You ain't ready."

Gwen walked over to him and handed him a cup of coffee.

"Jesus loves you for that. Yes he does. He don't like those shoes with that dress, now, but He forgives."

Gwen rolled her eyes. "They are character shoes. They kinda go with the whole theatre thing."

He dropped his sunglasses down and peeked over the rim. "Okay, friend, if you say so." He pushed his glasses back up and leaned over to Evelynn, who was sitting at one of the tables, as a co-conspirator, "Someone's a lil salty this morning."

Evelynn half-heartedly laughed and went back to her sketches.

Lucas cocked his eyebrow and furled his lip and looked at Gwen. He jerked his head back toward her and lifted his hands in question.

"Her ex."

Evelynn shot a look at her best friend as if she had been betrayed.

"Oh girl, it's no biggie. We all got exes." He took a few sips from his coffee and lifted his sunglasses up to prop them on top of his head. "This is the place? This where you gettin' married?"

"If he'll still have me."

"Oh girl, stop. That lil man loves you. I just talked to him last night and he told me to make sure you get whatever you wanted."

"He said that?"

Lucas held up his right hand, "Gawd is my witness."

Evelynn dropped her head on her hands and rolled it back and forth.

"Good gawd, what'd you do?"

"Nothing. Her ex just keeps trying to get her to meet with him again. He wants to talk her out of getting married."

"Well he can't," Lucas said matter-of-factly.

Evelynn lifted her head and looked up at the tall man.

"Obviously it's not going to happen, cause you'd have already done it and you wouldn't look like you had my hangover right now." He looked from one woman to the next. "I mean, seems pretty clear to me." He raised his eyebrows and was on the verge of saying, "duh". "Look, Pretty, we all make mistakes. You have to accept the past for what it is. You have to embrace the person you've become because of it."

Evelynn's eyes misted and she stood to hug Lucas and it was warmly received. "Aw, there now, you all better?"

She nodded and slid a finger under her eye to catch the tears before they ruined all of her make-up.

Lucas put his arm around her making her pivot with him and scanned the huge cavernous auditorium. "This room is amazing! I can see so many options!"

Gwen stood next to him and linked her arm in his and turned him toward the stage. "We were thinking having some chiffon over..."

"Oh yes! Chiffon, chiffon, chiffon, baby!" Lucas shook his head as if it was about to explode. "We can drape chiffon from the ceiling and loop in those rafters and make it look very Arabian!"

Gwen furrowed her brow and glanced back at Evelynn.

"Oh no... no... I see red satin... We can go for the Orient-look!" Lucas had pulled away and was off in his own world. He had a big empty room and an open-ended budget and was about to be eaten alive by his own creativity.

"For a wedding?" Gwen furrowed her brow.

"Well, we were thinking more along the lines of something simpler...?" Evelynn tried to interject.

Lucas stopped short and cocked his eyebrow while jutting his head to the side. "Girl, I am Lucas Lesley Powers. I am here to bring you a little bit of Paris, a hint of London, a dash of New York and try to make you forget that you're in lil bitty Bakersfield." He all but snapped his fingers before turning back to his previous thoughts.

"But, we *like* Bakersfield..." Evelynn attempted, but he was already gone. He had his notepad out scribbling madly.

The two women sat back down at the table and just let him wander. Every once in a while they'd hear a "Yes, baby, yes!" from somewhere in the theatre.

"What are we going to do with an Oriental wedding?" Gwen giggled.

"Maybe he'll come up with something different. We'll just let him get it all out of his system."

Gwen nodded. "Good idea."

Evelynn's cell phone chirped loudly.

"It's him! It's him!" Evelynn whispered loudly to Gwen. "What should I do?"

"Him who? Carlos? Again?"

"No! It's Dave! What should I do?"

Gwen shook her head confused. "What do you mean, what should you do?"

"I mean he's gonna..." The phone stopped ringing.

Both women looked at each other like they were hiding a dead body and almost got caught. "Whew, that was close," Evelynn sighed.

"What's the big deal. He doesn't know where we are."

"Yeah, but..." The phone rang again. "Omigosh! It's him!"

"Answer it!"

"Okay... okay." She took in a deep breath and pushed the connect button. "Hey... honey... what's up?"

"Hi, everything okay?"

Evelynn laughed a little too loudly and Gwen rolled her eyes. "Of course it is, why wouldn't it be?"

"No reason, I just tried to call a minute ago, and..."

"Oh, did you? I didn't hear it."

"Are you alright? You sound stressed."

"I am. Uh... I'm kinda in the middle of something and I really can't talk right now, so can I call you later?"

"Of course you can."

"Oh... why did you call?"

"No reason. I was just thinking about you," Dave said into the phone. Evelynn's heart melted... again. "I'll let you go. Call when you can."

"Okay..." Evelynn pushed the "end" button and leaned against a pole. "He called cause he was thinking of me." She couldn't stop smiling.

"Aren't you glad you answered it?"

"Yeah, I guess. I'm glad he didn't ask any questions though, I would have lost it."

Gwen laughed, "Yeah, I know. You are the worst liar! Now come on, let's go buy your fiancée a boat. Do you have the brochure?"

Evelynn dug into her bag and pulled out the top three. "Yep! He's going to be so excited!"

"If you can keep it a secret long enough! I bet you don't even make it till the wedding."

"You're on! Besides, we're just looking today!"

"I can't believe you bought the boat." Gwen closed the car door.

"I couldn't help it. It was such a great deal! And with them delivering it to his 'sloop' or 'skiff' or whatever it's called. It just seemed like the thing to do."

Gwen leaned over onto Evelynn's shoulder. "He's going to love it. You are such an awesome girlfriend."

Evelynn mirrored the pose and lay her head on Gwen's. "I am, aren't I?"

"Rip..." Nick took a bite of his cheeseburger. "What's up?"

Dave took his glasses and ball cap off and rubbed his face. "Nothin' man."

"Now..." Nick chewed and swallowed his bite. "I know that's not true because you 'd be halfway done with your sandwich by now. So... what's up?"

Dave pinched the skin between his eyes before slipping his glasses back on. "I think Evie is going to leave me.." He pushed his hair back and plopped his hat back on his head. "I think, she's going back to her ex."

"What? Dude, no." Nick put down his sandwich and wiped his hands before grabbing his glass of beer. "Has she said anything?"

Dave turned his hands up. "Really?" He picked at his seasoned fries. "It's not like they say anything ever. Like, 'I'm thinking about leaving you for my ex, you okay with that?' No," he dropped his head, "they don't SAY stuff, they... just do it."

"Okay, okay, back up." Nick pushed his plate to the side. "What makes you *think* she's planning on leaving you?"

Dave sighed heavily and looked away a little guiltily. "The other day, I was at her house and her phone went off. So, I went to grab it for her and saw that she had a new message from Carlos. That's her ex, right? So, I'm a little upset about that... I know, I know... I shouldn't think the worst, but then I see that there were four other texts from him!"

Nick closed his eyes and opened his mouth to speak, "I'm sure..."

"Wait, before you say anything, there's more. You know, how sometimes it shows that first part of the text? Well..." he looked away ashamed for reading it, "...it said *'mi amore'* That means *my love* in Spanish doesn't it?"

Nick furrowed his brow.

"Well doesn't it?"

"Yeah, it does, but you can't assume that..."

"Okay, I knew you'd say that, but... yesterday when I called her, she was acting all weird and you know... sketchy."

"Weird and sketchy?" Nick looked down his nose at his friend and pulled his plate back in front of him to tackle the other half of his burger. "Dude, you lost me. I may not have known Evelynn much longer than you but..."

"Dude... Nick,... help me out here!"

Nick stared at him blankly while he chewed.

"Please..." Dave pleaded.

Nick finished his bite and said, "Fine. Let's see if I can dig around in your paranoid little brain."

"This is serious. I love her so much I can barely breathe thinking she might leave me."

"Now there's a start. I may not know her very well, but you.... Have you told *her* that?"

Dave chuffed, embarrassed. "She knows. I asked her to marry me, didn't I?"

Nick rolled his eyes. "Rip," Nick scratched his eyebrow and ran his hand down his face. "Women like, sometimes *need* to be reminded that you love them. That you think they are beautiful... that... that she is the most important thing to you."

"And she is... all that stuff."

"Then tell her."

"I did! In the carriage ride, remember? I did and said all that stuff!"

"It's more than a one time thing, bud."

"Seriously?   I don't want to come off sounding like a pansy."

Nick rolled his eyes again.

"What? We can't all go around singing to women to win their hearts. Sensitivity looks good on you."

Nick laughed and shook his head, "What?"

Dave shrugged, "I'm just sayin..."

Nick took a drink from his frothy glass and laughed again. "The thing is," he got back to the main subject, "you don't have to win her. She already said yes..."

"That's my point!"

Nick closed his eyes and tried to gather his thoughts. "Like I said, it's not a ... one and done kind of thing. If you want this relationship to last... you want her to say 'yes' ... everyday, for the rest of your lives. You never stop trying to win her heart. Does that make sense?"

Dave shrugged and shrugged again feeling lost. "I'm just not... I dunno... mushy like that."

"It doesn't have to be mushy."

"I do nice stuff for her."

"Like?"

"Like, the other day I sent her flowers. She likes those."

Nick nodded in approval. "That is nice. And, bonus points for not reserving that move for when you get in trouble!" Nick teased.

They both laughed and fist bumped each other across the table.

Nick shrugged and added, "I think you should pray on it."

"Really? You're going to pull out the Jesus stuff? I came to you for help."

"I am helping you. A two legged stool won't stand."

"What the hell does that mean?" Dave was getting frustrated. He took of his ball cap and scratched his head. "Okay, fine... what... what does that mean. In language that I can understand, please."

Nick smiled. "That's exactly it. She needs a partner who is going to speak her language. Shares her beliefs."

"You know how I feel about that stuff. It's fine for you, but... it's just not... it's just not me."

"It *is* her."

"She's never asked me to change. She knows I can't get into all your rules and stuff, man. Life is too short to be told what I can and can't do by some "invisible eye in the sky." He fluttered his fingers for a spooky effect.

Nick rubbed his forehead searching for the right words. This subject rarely came up between them and he felt that he needed to say just the right things. But he didn't know what those were, so he just went with what his heart told him. "It's not my job to convince you or try to trick you into 'drinking the juice'."

Dave chuffed.

"For me," Nick continued, "when I became... saved? And I was forgiven of all my sins... it... *it* changed *me*. I wanted a different life. I was ready to look at myself in the mirror and see what was really there." Nick shook his head more to himself, remembering. "Those were hard days. I had a lot to fix in myself."

Dave looked at him incredulously, "You? You were practically a saint."

Nick furrowed his brow allowing for a brief moment the image of the man he used to be scurry across his thoughts. He pursed his lips and shook his head, "No. I wasn't." Nick tapped the table for emphasis, "But here's the thing. When I did... let go of the old me... I liked what replaced it."

Dave leaned in suddenly curious, "What replaced it?"

"A new me. A me with a clean slate. And it wasn't about rules, because I *wanted* to 'follow the rules' for lack of a better word. I was so grateful to have that old me gone, that I was, and am happy to show Him my gratitude. And He is faithful and renews that feeling in me every day." Nick looked up and saw Dave trying to grasp his meaning, "I don't know, it changed my whole life and I am happier for it."

Dave sat back and dropped his shoulders, "Yeah, well, I don't have burdens."

"Really? We're sitting here discussing the contentment you're feeling?" Nick nudged at his heart.

"She loves me the way that I am."

"So do I, but maybe she sees the potential that I see."

"Dude, you're flattering me, but I'm already spoken for." Dave laughed to lighten the mood. "You had your chance."

Nick smiled and chuckled with his friend.

A moment of uncomfortable silence hovered over the table and Nick finished off his drink before asking, "Okay then, ... has she been upset about anything lately?"

Dave rolled his eyes, happy that the conversation was back in *his* language. "Yeah, she's constantly bringing up my condo and wants to start house hunting. Then she wants me to go to church with her and stuff. I don't know those people. I mean, the wedding is like, I don't know, months away still."

Nick breathed out heavily already knowing where this was leading, "And?"

Dave clenched his jaw and looked away. "And... I haven't closed down the apartment yet." He attempted to shrug it off.

Nick scrunched his brows together, "What?"

"Dude, I've been busy."

"Really?   That's what we're going with, cause she's going to read it as... fear. Or... lack... of... commitment." He pointed his finger to invisible words in the Woman's Book of Life on the table.

"Thanks, Dr. Freud, it's not like my super ego isn't whispering that junk in my ear every day! 'What are you doing, Rip?' She's outta your league, Rip' 'Don't you see how amazing she is?' 'Do you really think you could make her happy compared to Carlos?'"

Nick shook his head, "Don't... don't do that. You seem to be forgetting that she chose you."

"Yeah?   Then why is Carlos calling her again?" Dave leaned back in his plastic chair and crossed his arms over his chest. "Dude, I've been selfish all my life. I know that. I'm the messed up child and my parents have literally bailed me out of everything." He leaned forward and tapped the table. "I've been irresponsible... my whole life. HOW am I supposed to take care of this woman who doesn't NEED someone in her life? Who... who is so amazing, but wants to have a family with me. ME! I'm thirty-six years old, man. I don't know the first thing about being in a real relationship. I'm freakin' out here, man. If I lose her... I don't.... I'll be lost."

"Is that why you're holding on to the apartment?"

Dave glared at him.

"No," Nick held up his hands, "I'm being serious. Maybe you're so busy thinking about having an escape plan that you're not... all in."

"All in? What... what's that?"

"Yeah, you know, all or nothing. If she's the one..."

"She is.

"Then you gotta go *all in.*" Neck leaned across the table and squeezed Dave's shoulder. "She needs to know that you are in this just as deep. That... no matter what- it's you and her. You got this, man."

Dave nodded, warming to the idea.

"And the church thing, that's her language. That's her wanting to share with you that God is in charge. If we let go and let God, our relationships will be stronger."

"Do you really believe that?"

"Absolutely. With all my heart. Pray. God will take care of the rest."

Dave looked at his friend skeptically.

"All in. If it's important to her, It needs to be important to you."

Dave nodded and picked up a fry only to drop it back on the wrapper.

Nick leaned back in his chair; "You got that other job, right? In Enterprise?"

Dave smirked, "Yeah, thanks to you. It will be a nice addition to the local stuff. Thanks."

Nick shook his head. "No need to thank me. Your work speaks for itself. I just... nudged." Nick tapped his empty glass. "Buy you another?"

"Nah," Dave shook his head capping himself off, "I've got some stuff to take care of."

"Good man." Nick smiled.

On the loveseat glider that sat on Evelynn's front porch, Dave sat with his arm around Evelynn's shoulder while he gently pushed it back and forth with his feet. Evelynn rested her head on his shoulder with her feet tucked underneath her.

"It's pretty nice out tonight, huh?" Dave offered.

"Mmm-hmm," she nodded un-committedly.

He could tell that she was bothered by something and he hoped and prayed that it wasn't what he was thinking.

He kissed her lovingly on the top of her head and spoke softly. "I'm going to have to leave soon."

She acknowledged the late hour, but still wrapped her arm across his chest. "I know."

He giggled softly, "You're not helping."

She laughed too, "I know."

"I hope you appreciate the effort it takes for me to push this swing with my short legs."

Evelynn giggled. "Do you want me to help?" She lifted to uncurl her long dancer's legs but he put his hand out to stop her.

"No, no... I want to take care of you."

She smiled and curled back in to the side of his body. They sat in silence for a moment more.

"You seem a little... uh... stressed these days."

Her immediate thought was, welcome to the world of an executive director of a theatre. She sighed out heavily. She had always thought she was better at hiding her stress but apparently she's not as good as she supposed. "I do have a lot on my mind," she admitted.

"How is Lucas working out? He's helping, right?"

Evelynn smiled. "He's quite a character. We all love him to pieces. Even Betty. He keeps her on her toes, though. He keeps us laughing, although sometimes I don't think he means to."

"Yeah, he's one of a kind, but he really does have a heart of gold."

"Oh he does. That's what makes working with him so... stressful."

"What does?"

Evelynn pushed against Dave's chest to sit up straight so she could see his face. "His ideas are amazing... but, they are just so..." she waved her hands in front of her as if she were trying to contain a cloud. "... so.... so... grandiose? I don't feel it's what either of us want, you and I, not he and I," she added for clarification, "but I just don't know how to tell him. He gets so excited."

"He's a good guy. I'm sure he'd understand."

"I don't know. I would just hate to hurt his feelings."

"Do you want me to say something to him?"

"Oh no... no..." she shrugged. "I mean, worse case, as of yesterday, it was 'green themed' and you would come out of a green castle and all I could think of was the *Wizard of Oz*."

"I am kind of a wizard," he smirked at her.

Evelynn paused for a moment but she couldn't contain the smile on her face. "Yes... yes, you are, honey. So I should tell him that it's a 'go' for your green tux then?"

"Uh... I'm gonna say no..."

"That's what I thought."

"I'd end up looking like a munchkin that was daring to walk next to the good witch, what's her name?"

She giggled, leaned in and kissed his cheek before tucking herself back into his side. "You're not *that* short," Evelynn said through giggles.

"So... uh... that's it then? Green tuxes?"

Evelynn shrugged against him. "More or less." She buried her nose into his neck. "It's getting chilly," she said changing the subject.

"Yeah... I guess." He ran his hand up and down along her shoulder to warm her. "Hey... uh... um... I love you, you know?"

Evelynn sat back up and looked into his eyes. She didn't say anything for a few seconds, but it felt like hours to Dave. Finally a smile tugged the corners of her lips and her eyes shined. "Thank you for that." She leaned in and kissed him and then kissed him again. "I know that you do, but it is so nice to hear. I really needed that."

She kissed him deeply and wrapped her arms around his middle holding him tightly. And for the moment, Dave was the happiest man in the world. Being a pansy wasn't so bad after all.

"Uh, excuse me..." Lucas waved his hands from the back of the theatre. "What are they doing to my stage! I need that space!"

Gwen caught him before he could railroad the set construction volunteers. "Here. Sit." She smiled at him and handed him his coffee. "We have an entire production to do before the wedding, and the sets have to be built for that first."

"But my castle..." Lucas whined.

Evelynn smirked. "If there's going to be a castle, then it's going to have to wait until after we strike the set of *Annie Get Your Gun*."

Gwen hugged his shoulders. "There's plenty of time. We theatre people perform short-term miracles all the time... it's how we're built." She laughed with Evelynn.

"Okay... good... I guess." Lucas slumped his shoulders and took a sip of his coffee, which was cooled since it had been sitting, and waiting on him for two hours. He pulled out his notebook and flipped it open and the girls watched his entire demeanor change. "Oh... girl... I was busy last night!"

Gwen cocked her eyebrow, "Aren't you always?"

Lucas laughed and leaned against her shoulder, "Mmm, girl, Y'all need Jesus... I meant with work... this time." He laughed again and turned his attentions to Evelynn, "Now, Princess, I have found a white horse a few counties over and we can use it for the day. I'm going to have it brought over early so I can..." He sat back in his seat and spread his hands out in front of him letting them know a big announcement was coming. "...put extension in his mane and tail. Can you see it?"

"A horse?" Evelynn asked.

"A white horse... a mystical horse..." he was lost in his own thoughts. "I wonder if we could put some body glitter on him so he'll sparkle." He jotted some notes in his notebook and didn't notice the look that Evelynn and Gwen shared.

Evelynn pinched her forehead and wondered how her simple, winter wedding got so derailed.

Lucas stood as he continued with his details, "And we'll have spotlights here, and here... and then glitter along the main aisle. You know, I'm sure they make a glitter machine. They have one for paper... I wonder.... " Another note written with a tiny little pencil in his tiny little book. He looked back up seeing the whole event in shining, glittering splendor. "And then, you will come riding in from the back, and... Oooo!" He stopped abruptly. "Who is that tall drink of water?" He spoke over his shoulder to the women sitting behind him at the table. "I call dibs!"

Gwen rolled her eyes, "I wish."

With the sun shining behind him, a lean silhouette stood in the doorway of the theatre. His black hair was slicked back with just a tendril slipping from it's otherwise perfectly gelled state. His shape showed his muscular form and his confident, movements.

Evelynn sighed and pushed herself away from the table. "You don't want this one." She walked up the center aisle. "What are you doing here, Carlos?"

Lucas gasped and turned to Gwen for confirmation, "The ex?" he whispered conspiratorially.

"It is."

"Oh, he's so beautiful. I'm really gonna hate having to beat him up if he hurts my girl..."

Gwen couldn't help but smile at Lucas' protection. But then also secretly wished for such an event.

"Please, my Angel, I must speak with you. It's life or death. If you have ever loved me..."

"Oh, he's good..." Lucas covered his mouth with his fingertips.

Evelynn walked past Carlos and out the door in which he came. Carlos turned and followed.

Dave couldn't stop smiling. He walked out of the Farmer's Market with a bouquet of fresh cut, fall flowers. He even leaned in to smell them before closing himself into his Ford Tempo.

He picked up the 8.5 x 11 piece of paper in his passenger seat and looked it over. He smiled again. "All in," he said to no one but himself.

The condo had sold and its contents were being packed up, right at this moment. They just needed a final address to send it to. He didn't want to presume so he didn't give them Evie's address. "Guess we're going house hunting." He turned over the key in the ignition, and the car purred to life. "I think I want a garage."

Evelynn pushed through the theatre doors to the outside. The sunshine outside was deceiving, normally leading her to believe that all is right with the world, but today... her ex-husband challenged her theory. Once she heard the door close behind her, knowing that Carlos was standing there, she turned on him. "What. Carlos. What?" She lifted her hands and then dropped them exasperated at her sides. "I told you that I didn't want to see you again."

"I hear your words, mi amor, but I know you. I know you deep inside you. You are just angry at the moment. You will forgive me, tu me sigues amardo... you still love me."

"No, I will forgive you because I don't need this extra baggage on me! I will forgive you because I am not going to let you control my feelings and thoughts any more. I will forgive you because this is the last time you are going to give me anything TO forgive you for! So, I forgive you. Are you happy now? Can we be done here, because I have things to do. I have a wedding to plan. *A wed-ding.* Do you hear me?" She moved toward him to get to the theatre door.

"Mi amor, your words hurt me. You won't even give me a chance to tell you..."

Evelynn looked down at the ground. "I don't love you anymore, Carlos. I have moved on. You have hurt me so many times and I don't understand why I kept taking you back... but now..."

"It's because you love me. And you know that our souls are meant to be together... Tu eres los latidos de mi corazon."

She looked blankly at him before speaking. "I'm done. I'm ready to move on."

He reached out for her and she smacked his hand away taking the chance to move past him to get back to the door. He grabbed her hand and spun her around to face him and wrapped his hands around her waist.

She pushed away from him, stepping back bumping up against the brick wall. "Don't do that!"

He paused and held his hands up in surrender. She massaged her forehead.

"Please... just hear me, my Angel... ten minutes...then I will go." He closed the gap between them.

She covered her face with her hands and shook her head. "No, Carlos... no more minutes, please... please, I'm begging you... just go."

He saw his opportunity and leaned in to put his arm just behind her against the brick wall. He touched her shoulder. "I will go... but I need just one favor from you por favore."

Dave pulled up on the office side of the theatre. He got out and walked around to the passenger side to get the flowers and the confirmation fax.

He closed the door with his elbow and started for the office. He saw movement at the front of the theatre and headed that direction instead.

He followed the sidewalk around the corner and stopped short. He saw his fiancée leaning against the wall and a man leaning in very, very close to her. It was a very intimate scene and Dave's skin pricked.

The flowers fell from his hand and hit the ground. It was happening. His worst fears... his feet were frozen on the sidewalk until she looked up at him. Guilt. It was all over her face.

He swallowed hard and turned to walk back to his car.

"David!" he heard her calling to him, but he couldn't... wouldn't stop.

"David! Wait... please!"

He opened his car door. His lip curled up in disgust as he watched her half walk, half run towards him. He took the piece of paper and smashed it into a ball before letting it fall to the pavement.

He started his car and pulled away.

What he didn't see were her fists balled up in rage or the tears streaming down her face.

What he didn't see as he drove off was her body crumbling to the ground crying, attempting to pick up the scattered flowers one by one. And when the man came to help her to her feet, what he didn't see as he sped down the highway was her unleashing decades of fury on that same man who was responsible for destroying her happiness. For all the years. The past until the present. Right now. This moment. As Carlos set her on her feet, she slapped at him as many times as her blind rage would make contact. She knew it was childish but she couldn't stop. He backed away guarding his face but she hurled her flat open hand against his body wherever it would make contact until her wedding planner picked her feet up off the ground.

Gwen grabbed the flowers and followed Evelynn and Lucas inside the office doors. Gwen turned back toward Carlos and spoke coldly, "If you are still here in ten minutes, the police will be hauling you away in handcuffs. Do I make myself clear?"

Carlos nodded and put his hands up in front of him and backed away.

"Money! That's all he wanted! He didn't come back because he loved me! He didn't miss me! He missed my money!" Evelynn was screaming and pacing in the office between the desks.

They let Evelynn rant and cry and pace while Gwen looked out the window watching Carlos go toward his car. Betty was ready by the phone and Lucas just handed Evelynn as many tissues as she needed when she walked past him and responded with the supportive, "Yes, girl," whenever it seemed necessary.

"I have to go find him. I have to explain..."

"Just wait one more minute or two and let yourself calm down." Gwen advised leaving her post at the window.

"You don't want to find him lookin' all a mess," Lucas offered another tissue.

Evelynn flopped down in an office chair. "What have I done?"

Betty, always the mother came and stood in front of Evelynn. She took a tissue from Lucas and lifted Evelynn's chin. She began wiping the tears from her cheeks and eyes. "You didn't do anything wrong," Betty dabbed. "The timing was just very bad."

"I know," Evelynn squeaked.

"You're going to calm down, go wash your face and then go explain everything. Just be honest. He loves you. He wants to believe you. He's hurting because his gut reaction said 'betrayal'."

"But I didn't..."

"I know, honey... and as soon as you can speak in complete sentences, you can go tell him that."

And then, at that moment, Nick, Dave's best friend, came through the office door.

"Hi, honey," Gwen called out to him.

He walked over and picked her up off the floor into a deep embrace.

Evelynn watched the interaction and the bawling began again. She grabbed a tissue and headed back for her own office.

Nick set Gwen back down on her feet and tugged his head toward her best friend. "What's with her?"

"It's been a tough morning," Gwen looked around the room absent-mindedly.

"Anything I can do?"

"Maybe... not just now though. What's up?" Gwen was torn as where to be. She felt she needed to be with her best friend but then she also needed to be here with Nick, who rarely came to the theatre anymore since his parent's died in a car accident earlier in the year.

"I... uh.... Could I talk to you for a minute?" he asked squeezing the back of his neck.

"Of course. Are you alright?" she reached out and put her hand on his arm.

"I... uh, yeah... but could we maybe..."

Gwen looked back at Betty who nodded, and Gwen and Nick exited the main office to go sit outside on a bench.

"Lawd, lawd!" Lucas slapped his thigh and rolled his eyes. He palmed his forehead and hiked his hip onto the edge of one of the desks. "There is more drama goin' on up in this joint than in my soaps!"

Betty smiled humbly, "Never a dull moment..."

Chapter Seven

Nick sat down on the bench just outside the office's doors. He leaned forward and rubbed his face before speaking. "I just can't do this anymore..." Nick began.

"Wait... what?" Gwen was already on edge and was trying not to think the worst.

"I am bored to death."

Gwen sighed heavily, relieved that Nick wasn't going to speed off down the highway behind his best friend and leave her crying too.... Or maybe he was? Her brain instantly scattered in a million directions. Was this his way of telling her that California was calling him back and his days of small town life were numbered? Was this him telling her that he had waited for her long enough? She attempted to sit quietly on the bench beside him. His elbows on his knees, he lifted his hat from his head, rubbed his scalp and put his cap back in place.

Gwen sat patiently, waiting for his next words... which were taking too long, so she asked, "I thought you were busy."

"I am." He shrugged.

"You are... too busy?" she coaxed.

He shrugged again. "I don't know." He leaned back on the bench and folded his arms across his chest. "I think I am just busy with the wrong things."

She placed a hand on his thigh and scooted in closer.

"I work the fields all day. Then I go home..." he swallowed hard, "to my empty house and... my parents are everywhere. Their things. It's my mom's kitchen. It's my dad's den. And I can't...bring myself to..."

Gwen rubbed his thigh in understanding. After his parents' death, they had tried to clean out some of their things, but he just wasn't ready. It was a painful adjustment for him and Nick's siblings had left him to the job.

"What can I do to help? Do you want Erin and me to come over tomorrow and we can start on one room?"

"I don't know. I know I should say yes, but I... I just can't make myself." He took a deep breath and leaned forward back to his knees. "I just don't feel useful."   "Maybe, you're lonely?"

He looked at her, questioning her statement.

"You're used to being around people... all the time. Having a top rated television show, a busy schedule, adoring fans... And now... you've settled into a quite, hard working, lifestyle that is..."

"...just what I asked for..." he finished the sentence for her.

"Babe, it's an adjustment."

"I'm not adjusting." He frowned.

Gwen swallowed but pressed forward. "Did you..." she cleared her throat. "Are you... thinking of ... going back?" There. She said it.

"Do you think I should go back?"

Gwen looked up to the sky for guidance but then spoke from her heart. "Selfishly, I don't want you to go back..." She paused, and swallowed hard knowing that she would be completely devastated if she had to live without him. They had come so far in the short year they have been in each other's lives. She almost robbed herself of happiness because of her stubbornness and now that she has felt what love is supposed to be, she couldn't imagine having to go back to her old way of life. And then suddenly, everything became clear to her and a calm came over her. She turned her head to look at him before she spoke, "... because then Erin and I would have to go with you and we'd leave Evelynn and Dave and the theatre... and... I ..." she chocked on her words try as she might to keep the emotion from them.

"You'd go with me?"

She pushed his shoulders back so he was sitting up again. She took his hand in hers, "Yes. If you wanted us, we would be there."

"I can't imagine my life without you now," Nick spoke barely above a whisper.

"Then we would go." A tear slipped from the corner of her eye as her brain started racing in the direction of all that meant for her life and all the changes they would have to make and all the people they would leave behind.

Nick slapped his thighs and stood up. "I know what I need to do next then."

Gwen felt the words get stuck in her throat. "What's that?"

"Find a way to feel useful."

Gwen smiled and shook her head. "You are useful."

"I know where you are going with this, but I feel I need to be doing more."

She conceded and nodded, "How about volunteering?"

He clicked his tongue and shook his head. "Tried that, remember? It was a disaster. People... fans started showing up and made a mess of the homeless shelter and..."

"... and the lines reached around the block for free soup you were ladling." Gwen snickered.

Nick shrugged. "I'm glad that I have such a presence, but I wish I could use it in a different way... Like..." he stared off across the parking lot. "It'd be great if all those people who showed up for the free soup, would have brought more soup... or signed up to help the next week, or started washing the dishes or cleaning up the place."

"Then show them. Give them a task to do. Maybe all they need is a little guidance."

Nick furrowed his brow, deep in thought.

"Around that same time, didn't we come up with a list of things... pay-it-forward things that we wanted to do..."

He nodded recalling a list of some sort...

"Why don't you start there?" Gwen nudged him further. "Only... instead of doing the work for a group or individual, get them involved... maybe?" She shrugged her shoulders resting her idea at his feet to run with it or trip over it.

Nick sat quietly for a moment more before a smile spread across his face. Just seeing it made Gwen smile as well. She loved his smile.

Nick reached out and cupped Gwen under her chin. Drawing her close to him he kissed her gently on the lips.

"I think I'm in love with you."

She giggled and kissed him again. "That's good, because I know I'm in love with you."

He stood up and stretched, his shirt lifting up to reveal a glimpse of his tanned stomach. Gwen looked down shyly but smiled.

She stood up behind him and crossed her arms in front of her comfortably. "Did you want to grab some lunch?" Gwen offered.

"Nope. I have things to do." He looked back over his shoulder and raised his eyebrows, "Useful things."

She laughed. "Good. Guess you'd better get to it then."

Nick was about to walk down the sidewalk to his truck when he stopped and stuffed his hand in his front pocket. "Oh yeah, I almost forgot... there's one more thing. I got a little something for you."

Nick tossed a small turquois box over his shoulder at Gwen. She caught it and looked questioningly at him.

He turned back around and flashed his Emmy-winning smile at her.

She covered her mouth with her hand and fell back on the slatted wooden bench. Tears filled her eyes. "Is this...?"

Nick walked back over to her. He picked up her empty hand and kissed the back of it and turned it over and kissed her palm.

"You are the best thing that has happened to me. I don't want to wait any longer. I want you in my life. I want your presence in my... our house. I want to make new memories with you..."

Tears were pouring down Gwen's cheeks as she listened to him. "Here? You want to stay here? In Bakersfield? Not California?" She could barely get the words out for crying.

"Anywhere you are, is where I want to be." He got down on one knee in front of her, "Gwen, I want to marry you." He held up his hand before she could speak. "I know we have to let Evie go first and I'm okay with that. But I want you as my wife at the earliest possible moment."

Gwen dropped down, kneeling in front of him. She wrapped her arms around Nick's neck and hugged him. She buried her face in his neck and kissed it as he wrapped his arms around her waist.

"Aren't you even going to open it?" he whispered, unable to mask the huskiness and emotion in his voice.

She pulled back so she could see his face and covered it with kisses. Her tears made both their faces wet. He wiped his face and then hers. "So? Is that a yes?"

She laughed and said, "I don't know... let me see the ring first."

He threw his head back and laughed. "Oh, I see how this is going to go..."

She pulled back the hinged top to see a classically styled engagement ring. It was not big and bawdy like you might expect from a rich and famous tv actor, but it was delicate and simple... elegant. The center square shaped diamond was surrounded by a swirl of smaller diamonds encased in yellow gold. It looked like something her grandmother would have worn. Her eyes darted from the ring to his eyes and back again. "It's so beautiful."

"I didn't want to get you anything too big because, you're a working girl and all... and I thought that if you wanted a flashier one, we could..."

She silenced him with a kiss. Her hands held his face still as her lips pressed against his. He attempted to speak through the kiss, "So... is that a yes?"

"Stop talking and kiss me."

He smiled, "I think she likes it..."

For the next two days emotions rolled and coiled around each other as each person knew it was best to stay quiet.

Lucas made himself scarce, Gwen kept her ring hidden and Nick gently tiptoed in the middle.

He heard the story from Gwen's side. He heard the story from Dave's side. Nick could clearly see where the wires got crossed, but now it's just a matter of Dave setting his pride and misconceived notions to the side.

On another note. Strange how when word of the drama made it's way back to Gillian's fiancée, Tom, Arkansas state trooper, that a few miles out of town Carlos was pulled over and ticketed for speeding, not wearing a seatbelt, not using his blinker, expired license plates, no insurance and no valid I.D.. He may be incarcerated for a while.

Evelynn tried and tried to reach Dave by phone to no avail.

Finally, Evelynn made her way to Stanton State Park and felt foolish for trying any other route prior to this. She looked first at his favorite picnic spot, but her eyes saw a defeated form sitting near the middle of the pier.

Evelynn took a deep breath and made her way down the pier. He lifted his head acknowledging the approach of someone, but made no effort to engage.

She stood beside him for a few moments not knowing what to say, and then finally, she knelt down in front of him and placed her hands in her lap. Dave took in a deep breath struggling to keep his composure as he responded to her presence.

They sat quietly as Dave broke apart pine twigs into little pieces and threw them towards the water. They rarely made it and created a dusting of pine pieces near the edge of the pier.

Dave pointed with a nod of his head to the left of him. "Somebody took my slip," he pouted.

Evelynn had to look away attempting to guard her secret.

"My favorite boat, too. Can you believe that?"

Evelynn swallowed hard. Does she tell him that it's his boat? Does she let him believe he's actually sitting here staring at someone else's boat?

"Uh..." she began, but he cut her off.

"Are you here to tell me you are leaving me?"

Evelynn's heart sank. "Oh, honey, no..."

"Look, I know why you would go back to him..."

"No... no, honey, I don't want..."

"Evie. I saw you. I saw you with my own eyes."

"I don't mean to sound cliché, but it isn't what it looked like." She looked up to his face but then dropped her head before she could continue. "I do owe you an apology though."

Dave clenched his jaw and shook his head. A lump settled in his throat as he did his best to brace for the worst.

"I should have shared my trouble with you. I should have told you that Carlos was trying to get in contact with me. I should have included you, and I am sorry for that." Evelynn's eyes burned and she swallowed hard, guilt washing over her. "But he is gone now and I don't think he will ever be back."

"So nothing happened is what you're trying to tell me?" Dave spoke harshly.

Evelynn swallowed but there was just air. Her mouth went dry, yet she pressed on. "There was a... um... a kiss." She reached out her hand to place it on his and he pulled it from her. "I'm sorry. It was an accident. I didn't mean for it to happen."

Dave pursed his lips, quivering with anger. "And?"

"He came to the theatre and started dancing with me. At the end of the dance, he... he kissed me."

"And I'm supposed to believe that's it?"

Evelynn pulled back and sat up straight at his stinging words. "Yes. Yes you are."

Dave chuffed. "And why's that?"

"Have I ever given you any reason to doubt my word?"

"This is different."

"No, it's not. It's my integrity on the line."

Dave's eyes dipped to hers briefly. "I believe you. I'm sorry. I just don't understand why... don't I... "

"I'm so sorry this happened. He just knows how to push my buttons... knows exactly what to say... "

"What does he say?"

"He... he tells me... I'm beautiful... and he... he just says nice things that made me feel... special... and I'm sorry... I... "

"I feel that for you. I uh, I think you're beautiful... don't you already know?"

Evelynn's eyes dipped low. She shrugged her shoulder. "No, honestly... I don't know. When I think you are giving a compliment, I'm not sure if you are teasing or being sincere."

It was Dave's turn to look away, feeling guilty. Nick was right. His eyebrows came together in deep concern and seriousness. "Well, I do." He tucked his hand under her jaw and stroked her cheek with his thumb. "If I haven't told you that you are the most beautiful and amazing woman that I have ever met, it's because I'm afraid you'll finally see that it's true and wonder what you're doing with a schmo like me."

She smiled but kept her eyes low.

She shook her head, wondering how they could have gotten so far off track in such a short window of time. "The reasons that I have to keep you and nurture our relationship far outweigh the list that you're creating in your mind of why I wouldn't. I love you. And I love what we are becoming. And I love the potential of what we will become in the future. We both have full lives behind us that may sometimes slip into our present, but that doesn't change the way I feel about you. Those things are behind us for a reason. I don't want them back. I want you. I want us."

Dave chuffed and smiled.

"What?"

"Nick said you'd say that stuff."

She smiled and shrugged her shoulders. "He and I speak the same language. We see things the same way."

Dave furrowed his brow as an unfamiliar feeling tugged at his heart.

"Evie," he continued, "*you* make me want to be a better man. I know I was living a bachelor's life. Irresponsible. Non-committal. But... you *see* me. Not for who I was, but for who I am capable of being. You believe in me. And I want to be that man that you see."

Dave pulled back and leaned against the back of the bench. He took a moment to massage the back of his neck and take a deep breath to keep the emotions from overwhelming him. Evelynn stayed silent and allowed him to continue at his own pace.

Finally, he took another deep breath and spoke again, his voice cracking with emotion. He slid from the edge of the bench and knelt down in front of Evelynn turning her toward him. He took her hands in his, "Maybe I didn't do this right..."

He took his hands back from her and wiped them on his pants, "Sorry.... Sweaty...."

He took her hands back in his. "I owe *you* an apology. I didn't do my job in never letting you doubt how I feel for you."

He took in another deep breath and blew it out in quick bursts like he was preparing for a race."

"Evelynn St. Laurence, you have changed my life. You have brought a light into my life where I never believed I could find one. You are so much more than beautiful. That's only the surface. I'm moving across the country to be with you because I never want to be without you again." He paused and rolled his eyes. He took his hands back and wiped them on his pants again. "I'm not good at this words stuff and I... I guess I took it for granted that you could see my heart. I'm sorry. I want to be your husband more than anything." Dave swallowed hard and a tear slipped from his eye. "You are so beautiful inside and out and I have to pinch myself every day that you are with me. You're my girl. You chose me. I love you... more than anything. More than... than food." They both laughed. She turned loose of his hand to wipe the tear from his cheek and then from her own. "Evelynn, would you... would you... do me the honor of becoming my wife on December second of this year? It would make me the happiest man on earth. Please, please marry me." The tears began to flow freely. "You will never have to doubt my love for you again."

Evelynn dipped her eyes down shyly, but a smile spread across her face. She stretched out her dancers body and threw herself into Dave's arms knocking him backwards on the dock.

"Yes, David Ripke. I will. I will marry you and I will never second guess your love for me again." She pressed her lips to his and wrapped her arms around his neck.

He wrapped his arms around her waist and buried his face into her neck. "I love you so much. I am so sorry."

Evelynn pulled away from him by straightening out her arms. "Oh, my love, You have no reason to be sorry. It was my insecurities and my doubts. I didn't mean to hurt you and I am so very sorry that I doubted us for even one second."

She leaned back down onto his chest and kissed him deeply, tangling her fingers in his hair. "It will never happen again." She kissed him again.

When Dave came up for air, he lifted her light torso off of his own. "Okay, you're going to have to stop that." He was breathing heavily.

She pushed against his arms causing them to buckle bringing her back to his lips for another kiss.

Dave slid out from underneath her, "Seriously, woman... if you want me to wait till the honeymoon, you really need to quit that." He lifted her from the dock to her feet. "You can't just do that to a man... I... I can't be held responsible!"

She laughed as she watched him walk in small circles on the dock. He sat back on the bench and readjusted his hat. She smiled and came to the bench and sat beside him and tucked his curls behind his ears. "You need a haircut. Want me to make an appointment with Rae for you?"

He shrugged. "I guess."

She turned his face toward her and smiled at him. "We are okay?"

He understood now that there was nothing he wouldn't do to keep and grow the relationship he had with this woman.

Evelynn furrowed her brow at his change of demeanor. "Are you alright?"

Dave nodded. "I don't blame you for doing what you did."

Evelynn swallowed hard, feeling the guilt fresh once again.

"I wasn't the man you needed me to be. But, I will be. I don't want to lose you. Don't give up on me."

"I'm not going anywhere. You are the one that I choose. We will grow together."

"I'm not going anywhere either. Except to eat. I'm starving. You want some fried chicken?"

A smile peeled across her face. She ran her fingers along the side of his head and tugged his hair. "I do. I do want some chicken."

He stuck out his arm for her to hook into and started walking down the pier. "Can you believe someone took my spot? I'm so mad right now."

Evelynn stayed silent.

"Oh, hey, can I meet you at the cars? I forgot something."

"Dave Ripke, don't you dare untie that boat!"

"Actually, I wasn't even thinking like that, but it's interesting to know where your thoughts go. There's an evil side to you, Miss Evelynn St. Lawrence. I like it." He smirked at her.

"Not for me! I was thinking about you!"

He nodded, "Of course you were, protecting your man... I won't do anything bad. I'll meet you at the car... I'll only be a minute." He bobbed his head encouraging her to walk on without him and he watched her reach the end of the pier before turning back to the bench he recently vacated.

He sat on the bench and leaned over to put his elbows on his knees and folded his hands. He sighed heavily and stood back up and paced in front of the bench.

He wandered over to the boat tied to the pier. "Stupid boat. I hope they enjoy it." He rolled his eyes. He walked to the water edge of the pier and looked down into the muddy water that sloshed against the moorings. "Okay, Lord... or Jesus... or... or uh, God... I really love that woman. And... and I want to be the man that she sees in me. And... I ... uh... I need Your help to do that." He pulled his hat from his head and straightened his hair suddenly feeling dirty. He rubbed his face and pinched the bridge of his nose to hold back the tears that were stinging. "I... I don't know how to do this stuff. I don't know what to say. But... she says if I call out to You, that You will hear me. So... uh, this is me, Dave... uh, Ripke. I need You... in my life. I want... I want that peace she has. I don't deserve it, but... uh, Lord... if You could find room for me, I am willing... no... I mean, I want You in my life. In our life, I want a three legged stool." He paused and took in a deep breath releasing the weight that he was carrying. "I ... uh... thank You. Thank You. Thank You for her. I'll do right by her, I promise."

Dave paused for a moment waiting for... something. He breathed in and smelled the water in the air, the pine scent wafting around him... the river was calm, peaceful... his heart was light. He couldn't help but smile. He cupped his curls behind his ears and pulled his hat back on his head. He nodded to the invisible presence, and smiled, satisfied that his words were heard and accepted.

The musicians began to make their way to the front of the church, which was the signal for the attendees to find their seats, as the service was about to begin.

Evelynn scooted into the pew next to Gwen and Nick. She sat and looked through the program while her neighbors chatted.

Gillian leaned forward from the pew behind and spoke softly to Evelynn, "The man in the navy blue suit and red checkered tie..." she let her words hang giving Evelynn time to spot the person of interest. Evelynn nodded, prompting Gillian to continue. "He's the new owner of the gym on Kelley Street. Ed Davis." Evelynn tipped her head back processing the information. "He wants to talk to you about sponsoring *Annie Get Your Gun.* His wife, Diana, is over there, getting ready to sing with the choir and he has a daughter... who can sing."

Evelynn looked over her shoulder, raising her eyebrows. "That's good news."

"And... he, was a fan of theatre back in high school. Maybe with a little nudge he would make a great Charlie Davenport or Sitting Bull."

Evelynn looked at the unsuspecting victim again. "Yeah, I could see it. Either one. We need to see what kind of involvement Roy is going to have with this production. I think he wanted Davenport."

"No, he wants Buffalo Bill Cody, remember?"

Evelynn smiled. "Then Mr. Davis would be a perfect addition! Am I supposed to call him?"

"I'll introduce you after the service and then you can take it from there."

"Great! Ever the scout! I can't wait to get you more involved."

"Too busy with the kids and cows... in that order," she laughed.

Before Evelynn could respond, the drummer clacked his sticks together and the band launched into the first song of the day. The congregation was on their feet clapping, singing and swaying while moving back to their seats.

Evelynn felt someone approach the end of the pew and she instinctively looked down to scoot over to make room. When she raised her eyes to the new person, she looked into the eyes of her fiancé.

He looked unsure. Nervous. A little sick to his stomach. The most genuine smile spread across her face and filled her eyes with love. She looked him over and in a matter of seconds, she saw that his hair was cut, he was wearing a button down shirt instead of his many t-shirts, and a pair of jeans with the sticker still on the thigh. She laughed only slightly so as not to upset him, but reached down and pulled the sticker from his pants and crumpled it up in her hand. He rolled his eyes and tried to turn away. She turned his face back to her own and mouthed, "It's okay. I'm glad you're here."

She tucked her arm under his and drew him into the pew. She lay her head on his shoulder for only a moment and was soon drawn back into the music.

"You guys have a band?" Dave loudly whispered.

Evelynn smiled and kept singing.

Nick reached across the two women and shook his best friend's hand.

Tom followed suit from the pew behind and Gillian embraced the new comer.

Dave had never felt more warm and welcome at any other time in his life.

He turned his attention back to the front as others patted his back and welcomed him as they passed by.

He bobbed his head, closed his eyes and fell into the music. Evelynn checked him out from the

corner of her eye and could not contain her smile.
"Thank You, God. Thank You for bringing him into
Your fold. You are amazing, You are wonderful,
You are a healer…"

Chapter Eight

"Well, hey there, sunshine!" Gwen cooed. "You've been scarce around here lately."

Lucas shook his head, "Girrrrl, y'all have way too many childrens around here all of a sudden."

Evelynn and Gwen laughed, "It's kinda what we do here," Evelynn offered.

"And that's a beautiful thing for you all, but honey, Lucas don't mix well with the younger generation, if you know what I'm sayin'."

Both Gwen and Evelynn looked at each other trying to figure out the hidden meaning that he could be referring to, but came up with nothing.

"They's loud, honey." He pinched the bridge of his nose as if he were holding back the imaginary noise.

"Speaking of loud, we've missed you in church these last couple weeks." Evelynn teased.

Lucas tried to look offended, but ended up giggling and covering his face. "You ain't right, you know that?"

"Yeah, we had to sit through the entire service without someone yelling from the back 'Yes, Lawd!' or 'Thank you, Jesus!'" Gwen added to his fits of giggles.

"Speak it, Pastor!" Evelynn threw out.

"What can I tell you, the spirit moves me." He cocked his eye feigning insult, "Y'all need Jesus. Imma here to tell you, y'all need some Jesus in yo life."

They were all laughing and Lucas wiped away the faux tear at his eye.

"So where have you been? Sincerely, you have been missed. Pastor Rogers didn't know what to do with such a quiet congregation."

"Yeah," Gwen laughed, "I could swear he would pause at the spots he thought you would call out and was so disappointed when you didn't."

"I think he... we enjoyed your being there."

"Well, honeys, I hate to pull the Brown card, but y'all don't know how to 'church'."

Gwen squinted and asked, "Now, when you say y'all..."

"Oh yeah, it's what you think. I had to find me a brown church. Girl, they know how to 'church'. "

"And when you say 'church'..." Evelynn air quoted the word.

"Girl, how am I supposed to explain..." He searched his mind for the right words and his face softened as a smile spread across his face. "I drive into the parking lot and follow the cars to the back lot, cause I'm always late."

Gwen nodded confirming his habitual tardiness.

He cocked his eyebrow and decided to ignore the silent judgment. "So, I'm making my way up to the front door... I can hear the choir in there singin'... and I am greeted by Homer at the front door, who must have forgotten that he was goin' to the house of the Lord for his tacky self was right there for all to see, shaken' hands; his mix matched clothes and nappy head."

Both girls shook their heads and rolled their eyes, but he was on a roll now.

"So I walk in, looking fabulous, I might add, and there is Miss Gilani, all huggin on people thinkin' she's the church leader with her nasty wig and her perfume, child... I can't even... I mean, I go two aisles around just to keep from her thinkin' she can touch me. Excuse me? I don't think so. Y'all with me?"

Evelynn and Gwen looked at each other not sure if he was asking them or still caught up in his reverie.

"The choir is singing, and Jesus forgive me, but you know how I am, these woman need to invest in some Spanx... you know what I'm sayin'? They is workin' those Maiden Forms, believe me. If one of those snapped loose, it could destroy a city. Y'all hear me? And I'm not mentioning any names, but I promise you that the soprano in the second row on the right, we know why she's singin and shoutin' and it ain't because of Jesus. He cocked his eyebrow again and tsked his lips, while the girls covered their mouth. "Mmm-hmmm"

Evelynn was laughing to the point of tears by this point and couldn't help but add, "I'm sorry, *who* did you say needed Jesus...? 'Cause..."

"But.... " he continued as if he didn't hear her, "...after we done prayin' and praisin', we get ta eatin'. Mmm-hmmm-HMM," he stomped his foot for emphasis, "Now, that's where Jesus gone be. Tastin' on some collard greens and some black eyed peas and turkey legs, child, you felt you died and gone to heaven. And you think y'all are doin' right by havin' your little "pot luck" dinners," he air quoted the word. He shook his head before he continued, "And... and here's what I got to say about y'all's pot luck. You think that you can put any old thing in a dish, bake it at 300 degrees for forty-five minutes and call it a casserole. Ya hear me?" He curled his lip and looked disgusted. "There ain't no telling what's in there under all that cheese. I ain't eatin' that... No sir."

The girls were laughing so hard that they could barely come up for air. Inspired, Lucas continued on his rant. "And if you think I was loud, honey, you wouldn't have been able to hear me at this church! If that preacher man be up there and doin' the Lawd right, that place be on it's feet!"

Gwen smiled, "And you found a good 'preacher man' did you?"

Lucas clicked his tongue and spoke out of the side of his mouth, "I don't know 'bout all that... but when I tell you they had some gizzards and some crawfish???" He stomped his feet and reached his hands out to the heavens. "Lawd, help me."

"Well, you are genuinely missed at the white people church." Evelynn composed herself and wiped away the tear under her eye.

"I thank you for that." He pulled the two women into an embrace.

"And," Gwen grabbed her phone and lit up the home page, "If you want to avoid the children, now would be a great time to vacate the premises. The school bus will be dropping them off in about fifteen minutes."

"Oh girl, I'm gone.   I'm sure I have something to do, somewhere else."

"On that note, what's new with my wedding? Anything I need to know about?"

Lucas scrunched up his face, "Baby, you can't rush talent. I got to stew on things."

Evelynn smiled, "Oh, of course,   my apologies."

"I forgive you.   I'll see you ladies tomorrow... maybe, depending on what the night holds. Toodles!"

"That's it. I'm done." Dave came bursting into Evelynn's office and flopped down on her chaise. "I'm going to be a sponge forever. I'll never have any of the nice toys."

Evelynn swiveled in her office chair to face him. He was laid back with his one arm and one leg hanging off the side as if he had just been shot and that's where he fell.

"Of what are you referring?" Evelynn asked calmly.

"Nick has all the cool toys!"

Evelynn raised her eyebrows, "Did you really just say that?"

He opened one eye and looked over at his bride to be. "He's going to go look at boats this weekend. Boats, Evie!"

"Really? Why is that a bad thing?"

"Cause then he'll have the boat and we will all go boating with him!"

Evelynn straightened in her chair. "Oh, I see what you mean. That would be awful! I would hate to know someone with a boat!"

Dave slouched and looked at her exasperated. "You don't understand..."

"Tell me," she coaxed.

"Nick has the nice house and the pool, so we go there, hell, oh, uh, I mean, heck, I'm living there! He has the big truck so we all ride with him. He's got the amazing grill, so we all eat at his place... I feel like a sponge! And now he's going to get the boat and then you'll say, 'there's no need for us to get a boat because Nick already has a boat and you guys do everything together anyway.'"

Evelynn covered her mouth trying not to laugh. "How do you know I'd say that?"

"Because you basically said the exact same thing about the house we looked at with a pool."

Evelynn shrugged, she couldn't deny it. "So is this a competition?"

"No... I would just like to have something that everyone comes to us to do."

"Does Gwen know he's going boat shopping?"

"Yes."

"And?"

"She asked him to wait. For what reason, I have no idea, probably something theatre related," he groused.

Evelynn snickered at her fiance's despair. "So, then what's the problem?"

He looked at Evelynn as if she was dense. "Look what happened because I listened to you! I waited and someone else took my spot! And my boat!"

"My love, there is more than one boat..."

"But that was my spot!!"

Evelynn didn't know what to say. He was sincerely upset.

"And you know what's even worse?"

Evelynn shook her head, waiting.

"He doesn't even use it!! I mean, it's been there for a flippin' month and he hasn't even taken it out! What's he waiting for?"

"Have you been stalking this poor boat owner?" Evelynn asked cautiously.

"No, but I can see it with my own eyes. He hasn't even made it seaworthy. There's stuff you gotta do to it before you take her out and he hasn't even done that."

Evelynn pursed her lips and looked everywhere but at her future husband, trying to keep her secret. "Maybe...," she began. "Maybe, he's just waiting for the spring? Maybe he's worried it will be too cold to..."

"Too cold?? We are in the best Indian Summer ever! And they are saying it's going to be a light winter, so there could still be MONTHS left to boat!"

"Oh... I didn't know."

"No, I'm sorry, honey. I don't expect you to know these things. I know you're busy with all your classes, but..." he sighed, defeated. "My job doesn't start until January and I am bored to death! And now, Nick is going to get a boat. And he and James are going to get Harleys and I'll just be here twiddling my thumbs waiting for a few spare moments with you so we can go house hunting." He slumped back down on the chaise and pouted.

Evelynn got up from her chair and walked over to the chaise. She looked down at the thirty-five year old toddler in front of her. She spoke with her eyes and Dave sat up and moved over so she could sit beside him.

"I'm sorry you are so upset," she coo'd.

He shrugged and kept pouting.

"You can still get a boat. We can find another sloop.'

"Slip."

"Right. Slip."

"I know." He took in a deep breath and released it. "Don't take this the wrong way. I am happy with my decision to move here. I love you and wouldn't change that for the world. But it feels like... nothing is mine. Not even you. I have to share you with so many people..."

Evelynn's face responded immediately.

"I am so proud of everything you have accomplished and I am so proud that people from miles around come to you because you are the 'expert' and you are so good at what you do... and plus you're just a really nice person, but... nothing about any of this says... 'me'. I'm not mad for waiting. Like you said, there are other boats, and other 'sloops'," he teased. "But I really thought that I had found... my... thing. My 'this-is-Dave's-boat', come on over and I'll take you for a spin...thing."

Evelynn put her arm around his slumped shoulders and kissed him on the cheek. "I love you, so much. I appreciate all that you have given up for me, so that we can be together here." Evelynn sighed out heavily. She stood and walked back to her desk rubbing her forehead in indecision. She sat back down in her office chair and ran her finger over her desk drawer hoping that something or someone would come in and interrupt them. The room was still quiet, and her fiancé sat sadly in her office. She had to fix it, right?

She slid the drawer open and pulled out a manila envelope. She went back and sat by Dave. "Here. It's yours."

She handed him the heavy envelope and he looked at her questioningly.

"I was going to wait until the Spring... until it was safer..."

Dave's eyes narrowed, not understanding.

"The instructions to make her sea-worthy are inside." She looked coyly up at him daring him to open the envelope.

He turned it over and folded up the clasp, lifting the flap. A set of keys fell out onto his hands. His eyes widened and his jaw dropped...

Evelynn leaned in to Gwen's office and peeked around the door at her best friend. "I might have done something that I wasn't supposed to do..."

Her interest piqued, Gwen sat up from her work and non-verbally requested more.

"You know that thing, that we bet on, that you said you would win..."

"Which thing?" Gwen laughed. "That happens on a weekly basis."

"A boat! A boat! I gotta boat! I am marrying the best woman on the planet! She got me a boooooaaaaat!!!!" Dave was running down the hall yelling and dangling his keys over his head.

Evelynn smiled, "That one."

Chapter Nine

All the classes at the Bakersfield Fine Arts Centre had been put on hold as the students were ushered to the auditorium for a "special news update".

The teachers and staff quieted the room by raising their hands as the large white screen was lowered from the ceiling of the stage and covered the black main curtain.

Gwen made her way to the stage and grabbed the microphone waiting for her and looked up at Miss Ashley, in the tech booth for confirmation to proceed.

"Hello everyone and welcome. I wanted to thank all of our students and parents for allowing this quick break in our class schedule to support one of our own. And Miss Ashley is telling me that it's just about that time, so I'll hand the controls back over to her."

Gwen replaced the mic and stepped down from the stage to sit beside her students. The lights dimmed and the sound cracked as the screen lit up showing the tail end of a Mark Everson Motors commercial.

A few seconds later, the smiling face of Monica Kelley, anchorwoman for the tri-state news station appeared on the screen.

"Today, we have a special treat for y'all." Through her thick southern drawl and raspy voice, you could hear a smile in her voice. "We've got a segment for you along the lines of 'Where are they now' and I'll tell ya, I'm happy to say that he's right here next to me," she laughed. "Now, y'all know him from *Real People, Real Lives* but he decided to leave us and take his life in another direction. So after five hundred episodes, and I promise you, I didn't miss a-one, he is returning to his fans, but this time, he's on the small screen and he's needing some help from you..." She turned her chair as the camera pulled back to reveal her guest. "Y'all, I am so excited to introduce you- back on television- where, personally, I think he belongs, Nick Penn everybody." She stood and Nick followed suit and accepted the warm embrace.

As they sat back down, Nick smiled, "Thanks for having me, Ms. Kelley."

"Oh honey, I've seen you in your skivvies," she flirted, "I think you can call me Monica."

Nick laughed as she explained to the audience the episode of his former series, "Our Nick here, was attacked by that huge bird and it literally ripped his pants off!"

Nick looked into the camera and pointed, "Ostrich farming. More dangerous than it looks." He cocked his eye passing on the warning to any ostrich farming wanna-bes.

Monica laughed heartily and leaned heavily against his arm. "Your show was always so entertaining. I just loved it. But I am intrigued with what you've got planned for us next. Before we get to that, what on earth have you been doing since you have dropped out of the spotlight?"

"Farming." He nodded and shrugged acknowledging the lack of star-quality in such an activity. And for emphasis, he added, "Corn and soy, mostly."

Monica's face reflected the lack of enthusiasm and Nick played off of it. "Exactly," he said confirming her reaction.

"We all expected you to be lounging poolside somewhere exotic..."

"Well, I have been working on that coveted 'farmer's tan'," he rolled up his sleeve and showed the stark difference of the ¾ tan sleeve and white shoulder."

She laughed. "But, now a little birdy told me that you've been busy locally here, in Arkansas."

He nodded. "I have. I got involved with the Bakersfield Fine Arts Centre and their live theatre. I had forgotten how much I loved it and how great it felt to have a live audience. The immediate love, instant gratification... it's unlike anything else for a performer. If it's funny, they laugh. If it's sad, I can hear it in the silence or a sniffle or two, but most of all," he reached out to touch Monica's arm, "It's the applause. It's like a drug. If you've done well, the audience will love you back immediately. And, oooo, if they don't they're not shy about letting you know that either!" he chuckled.

"Oh," Monica batted her hand at him. "You don't ever have to worry about that, I'm sure." She turned to the camera and smiled her signature smile. "Do y'all want to see some pictures?" She assumed that her home audience has answered 'yes' and proceeded. "Now, tell me what we're looking at here."

Nick looked over his shoulder. "That was *Camelot.* I was Lancelot and Guinevere was played by the beautiful and talented Guinevere Collins."

"You look good in tights."

Nick laughed, "As you know, it's not my first time in the 'tights arena'"

"The Avon sales lady!" Monica burst out laughing revealing the former series episode. "That was a hoot!"

"For you maybe!" Nick laughed along.

He followed her gaze as the picture changed behind them. It showed Nick Penn in a frumpy polyester dress, pantyhose and sensible shoes carrying an Avon bag bursting with goodies. He shook his head and covered his forehead.

"I had no shame..."

"But now this looks interesting. I love the cowboy motif," she teased.

"Ah yes, apparently it's all about the dressing up for me." He laughed. "This one is *Annie Get Your Gun.* It's coming up soon!" He leaned conspiratorially and "whispered" into the camera, "Tickets are now available!" He winked.

"And I see you are matched again with your favorite leading lady?"

Nick smiled, almost blushing.

"And," Monica continued, "rumor has it that you are going to make her your forever leading lady?"

Another picture popped up to show the smiling faces of Nick, Gwen and her adopted daughter, Erin.

In the theatre's auditorium, a hundred voices "awww'd" for their artistic director and fellow student.

Erin pointed to the screen, "Momma! Look! It's us! We're on T.V.!"

Back in the studio: "It looks like you've got everything you could ask for," Monica prompted.

"You'd think." Nick leaned back in his chair and took in a deep breath. "I've been a lucky man. I am very blessed, it's true. I just feel that I should be giving back. I don't think it's right to have built so much and not help others."

Monica nodded sympathetically.

"Here's the thing. I know that people need more than a hand out. That's a quick Band-Aid. I'd like to get out there and get involved with people and their communities instead of just clicking the 'donate here' button." He leaned forward raising his hands. "Now, don't get me wrong, we need funding and if that's how you are lead to give, then don't let me discourage you. But me, personally," he pressed his hand to his chest, "I want to get out there and work with the people and established organizations and make stuff happen. Instant gratification, you know?"

Monica smiled sincerely, "I love the sound of that. What can we do to help?"

"Well, Monica, I've put together this non-profit organization called *The Phoenix Project.* We are going to connect with select organizations, put out a call for help from the community, and see if we get these great causes some momentum in their efforts." Nick leaned forward again, the excitement building in him. "A lot of these organizations have to wait for corporate sponsorships or government funding and are so busy trying to fund, that they miss out on the 'doing', which in ninety percent of all these non-profits, that's where their heart lies. They created these groups to *DO*... to... to help, and so often they can't get very far. I'm hoping we can get in there and breathe some life, a little action and awareness to these groups. It may not solve all the problems of the world, but we can make a difference in *some*one's life, a little at a time."

"Well," she stretched out the word to a few extra syllables, "I've got to tell you, I just love hearing the passion behind your mission." Monica oozed her southern drawl across her words. "And if there is a man that can make things happen, I believe it could be you, Mr. Penn."

He smiled and shrugged, "Here's hoping."

"We've only got a few more minutes, so, I guess tell us what we can expect next."

"Well," he jumped in, "our first project is adding to the tiny homes community in Essex. I've sat in with their board of directors and we think we can get eight tiny homes built on acreage that has already been donated. And that will help eight veterans get back on their feet."

"Oh! I love it! I just love it!"

"So, we'll need carpenters, electricians, plumbers and all around handymen to help. We'll also need donations of supplies, if any businesses are looking for a healthy tax write-off," Nick winked at the cameras.

"Now what about those of us who don't know which end of a hammer to use?"

"We need help of all kinds in order to get the most amount done in a really short window of time. So, if you can paint, help clean, feed people; if you have a truck and are willing to gopher...I promise you, Monica, if you show up with a helping heart, we can put you to work."

"How do we find out more?"

"I'm glad you asked, Monica," Nick slipped into his professional, deep announcer voice and pointed to the screen behind him. The screen displayed a website, contact information, and every social media platform to reach for those who might just be able to help spread the word. "You can donate time, money, gifts, food... we want to see how much we can get done in a few days time."

"This is just great. I love it. And we'll be able to see your progress?"

"Absolutely! You know I work best when there's a camera man following me around," Nick laughed. "We'll have either weekly or monthly episodes that will air on Facebook and YouTube. We haven't quite worked out those details as yet."

"Well, well, Nick Penn, you have a big heart. I wish we had more time to talk about this, but promise me you'll be back with updates for us."

"I love our visits, Monica, and I'm so excited about *The Phoenix Project* and the reach it can have, so of course, it's an honor to be here with you. I am grateful for you having me here today and participating in this launch."

"Oh Nick, I'm sure I can safely say that we are all glad that you will be back in our lives on the small screen and the real lives you'll be touching is going to be worth the wait."

Nick smiled his Emmy-winning smile and added, "Hashtag *The Phoenix Project*"

"And there you have...."

The screen blacked out and faded to its original white. The auditorium lights came back up.

"What do you think, huh?" Gwen called out to the crowd as she ascended the stage steps getting the audience riled up. She grabbed the mic and spoke into it, "Do you think we can help Mr. Nick out on *The Phoenix Project?*"

A little girl raised her hand from the audience, "Yes, Kinzley?"

"Your picture looked pretty on the television."

Gwen smiled, "Thank you, sweetie."

"My picture was up there too!" Erin shouted from the third row.

Another hand went up, "Yes, Kerri?"

"Are we going to be on the list? We're a non-profit, right?"

Gwen nodded. "We are, but we had Mr. Nick all to ourselves last year and he really helped us out. So, now it's our turn to help others. But, I'm sure if we were in need, we could get put on the list," she winked and laughed.

"Can I get on the list? I'm in need," Miss Jenni called out teasing.

"We'll see what we can do," Gwen teasingly rolled her eyes.

"I am loving the choreography you did for the *I'm an Indian Too* number," Evelynn praised Gillian. "Your intermediate class is really coming along nicely. I bet they are excited for the recital this year. To have *Swan Lake* on your resume is quite a perk for anyone wanting to take their talent further."

"Thanks. They are enjoying the break from the strict movements of ballet to do something fun like this show. And true, taking on *Swan Lake* might have been a little more than I could chew, but they are working so hard and improving with every rehearsal."

"I can tell!" Evelynn retied her wrap-around skirt and looked over the reservation books on Betty's desk. "It looks like we're going to be sold out for opening weekend."

"That's awesome! You've got a really great cast. They have been such a pleasure to watch."

"I think it's going to be a good show. When does your next class start?"

"Not for another hour."

"Where's Gwen? I think we have the new student starting today... Robyn?" she scanned the hand-written attendance sheet.

"I believe she's in the auditorium with Lucas. Need me to go and get her?"

"Oh, no. By the time you'd get there, she'd be off and running somewhere else." Evelynn sat down at the end of Betty's desk and propped her feet up on the filing cabinet.

"How's Dave liking the boat?" Gillian asked.

"He loves it. Haven't seen him for days!" Evelynn laughed.

"What? Is he lost at sea?"

"No, no, nothing so adventurous. But he is at the dock every day learning more, cleaning, tying knots..." Evelynn shook her head and rolled her eyes. "This is what I see every day." She holds up her finger to pause the conversation and grabs her phone. She pushes a few buttons and hands the phone to Gillian. "I give you my message history..." she laughs.

Gillian giggles as she scrolls through the dozens of selfies of Dave on the boat, off the boat, near the boat, steering the boat, cleaning the boat, lounging on the boat, and others. But in every one, his smile is so big and cheesy that Gillian couldn't help but be happy for him. "He looks like he is having a blast."

"He must be. I'm glad I didn't wait until Spring." Evelynn leaned in so she could hush her tones, "And, it keeps him busy so I can put in the hours that I need to here."   Evelynn and Gillian laughed. "I know that sounds terrible, but…"

"No, no, I get it!"

Betty came in the office with a basket of towels to fold for the student lounge. "What are you two whispering about?"

"Keeping our men-folk out of our hair," Gillian confessed.

"Let me know if you need a few pointers!" Betty laughed out loud, tickled with herself.

"So," Guieneve stormed into the main office where the other women were taking a break between classes.   "Lucas is on the catwalk, checking out the support beams."

"That walkway by the lights?" Betty asked for clarification. "In the rafters?"

"Gwen nodded. "That's the one. Waaaaay up there where all the spotlights and things are."

Evelynn and Gillian exchanged glances, then Evelynn asked, "What's he doing up there?"

"Well," Gwen plopped down in Betty's office chair, "*Someone* just watched *The Greatest Showman*… with Hugh Jackman?" She looked around the room for their recognition, and all responded with nods.

"I love that movie," Gillian added. "The kids sing those songs all the time. It's a great movie."

"Yeah it is and suddenly Lucas thinks we should be doing those kinds of circus things for *Annie Get Your Gun*." She put her hand to her forehead, "I tell you, I love him to death, but he just wears me out!"

"Um... " Evelynn scrunched her face, "... the show opens in a week."

"Evie, the man has no concept of time."

And, as if on cue, Lucas saunters in the room. "Hello my lovelies!"

"Trapezes?" Evelynn cut to the chase.

"You think so too! I knew you would! It will be so great!" he gushed.

The ladies couldn't help but giggle. "No, Lucus. Not trapezes," Evelynn scolded.

Lucas pouted and looked at Gwen. "You didn't tell them the right way."

Gwen laughed, "I'm sorry. But I don't think there could have been a right way to tell them so they would have gone along with it."

Completely undaunted, an idea literally flashed across his face and the whole room braced to hear it. "I know!" he beamed. "The bearded lady! And it could be me!" He struck a pose and then drew his arms in with giddiness, waiting to hear the response. "I already have the beard!"

Evelynn laughed and shook her head. "Lucas, you can't be the bearded lady." She rubbed her eye, and looked away. "At least not for this production."

"But why?"

"Firstly, it's not in the script..."

"Yes, but..."

"Secondly, the show opens in seven days and we cannot throw new stuff at the cast and crew." Evelynn pushed the button on her phone to check the time and then walked toward her office.

"Where you going?"

"I'm putting my phone away and getting my ballet shoes back on because my students will be here soon."

She disappeared around the corner and reappeared with her ballet slippers in her hand.

Lucas huffed, "Girl, you is tight."

"Because I'm getting ready for my class?" Evelynn questioned.

"When was the last time you just had fun? I need to take you out."

Evelynn opend her eyes wide and raised her eyebrows in surprise. "Lucas, I don't think I'd survive a night out with you." She uncrossed her legs and pushed off her thighs to stand. "I don't even *know* what you do, but I do see you when you come in in the mornings... or rather, the afternoons."

Lucas threw his head back and laughed a high pitched squeal, "Girrrrl, you sho is right. You not ready." He leaned back against the desk shaking his head imagining her in some strange scenario only beknownst to him. "You not ready."

Evelynn heard her phone go off in her office but ignored it.

"Aren't you going to get that?" Betty asked.

"It's an unknown number, so I don't answer it anyway. Besides, I have a class in about ten minutes."

Just then, her phone went off again. And Gwen's phone chirped. Gillian's phone sang and the Studio phone lit up.

"It's Nick," Gwen looked down at her phone.

"Tom," Gillian looked at the others perplexed.

"Bakersfield Fine Arts Centre, this is Betty, how may I help you?"

"What?"

"When?"

"Yes, she is, can you hold please?"

Gwen's panicked eyes reached Evelynn's.

"Are you sure?" Gillian was saying behind her.

Evelynn felt like she was moving in slow motion trying to reach the phone in Betty's hand.

"Hello? Yes, this is Evelynn St. Lawrence. Wha...what? No... but... yes, yes, of course I can."

"Evie, I'm so sorry..."

"What? What?" Betty and Lucas were left out of the loop.

Evelynn handed the phone to Betty and stared off in a daze..."I... I have to go..."

"I'll drive you." Gwen said, taking Evelynn's hand.

"What's happened?"

Evelynn blinked and a tear dripped down her cheek. "Dave... he's been in an accident... They don't know how much time he has..."

Chapter Ten

The waiting room was quiet, but emotions were palpable. Nick sat and chewed on his thumbnail pretending to watch the cattle report on the corner television.

Evelynn paced back and forth frowning. She would stop at one end of the room or the other and close her eyes in prayer. Gwen sat in a corner chair with a stack of scripts next to her on the end table. The *Importance of Being Earnest* was folded open on her lap.

When Evelynn would stop in front of her, she extended out her hand for Evelynn to grab (or not) and join her in silent prayer or just to remind her that she wasn't alone.

The waiting was interminable. Testing. Testing. Testing.

Every time a human wearing scrubs entered the waiting area, every eye would turn in their direction hoping, willing that the news would be for them.

"Did you call Dave's parents? Evelynn stopped in front of Nick.

"I did. They should be here any minute, actually," Nick turned his wrist over looking mindlessly at his watch.

"I've asked you before?" Evelynn furrowed her eyebrows.

Nick smiled, "Only a few times. It's all good."

She pushed air out, tired, exhausted. "I'm sorry... and you're alright? Do I need to get *you* anything?

Nick shook his head, "Nope. I've been checked out and released."

She paced the room again and returned in front of Nick, "And James? Did we hear anything about James yet?"

He patiently shook his head again, thankful for the distraction, actually, "Not yet. They said they would be in... "

"Is Danni here yet?"

Gwen fielded this question. "She is, honey. She and Nina are in there with James."

"I'm sorry," she apologized to both. "I just feel so helpless."

The rose-colored walls and neutral furniture were designed to keep the guests calm, but Evelynn was restless. She needed answers. She felt fear in the unknown.

A surgical nurse came into the small room and scanned it silently before walking toward a young couple resting on a couch along the back wall. Evelynn sighed out heavily.

"Seriously?" A loud voice bounced off the walls outside the waiting room. "How do they expect you to find this place? Are they wanting me to walk the whole floor? These signs don't help at all." The voice got louder as it approached the room and the only one who recognized it, Nick, cringed and attempted both a silent warning and an apology for the upcoming visitor.

Both girls looked questioningly at Nick who neither had time to explain or hide.

A woman with short salt and pepper hair marched in the room carrying a purse on her forearm. She looked under her bangs, scowling at the room and the people in it. "Pffft... that coffee smells old..." she mumbled under her breath. She wore a flowered loose fitting blouse, black worn Capri's and sandals.

"Nicky!" she shouted from the doorway. "Is that you?"

Nick stood and braced himself for the interaction. "Mrs. Ripke, so glad you could make it. You didn't..."

"Look at you," she interrupted walking toward him. "My Nicky-boy," she patted him on the chest." "I've known this boy since he was in his teens," she spoke to either of the two women who came to stand beside him. "He's famous." She turned to tell a different, random stranger.

"Uh, Mrs. Ripke..."

"Hey, you can call me Helen. You're grown. You don't have to call me..." She jerked her thumb towards him and made a disapproving face, " You believe this guy? Calling me missus after all these years?"

Attempting to draw her attention back from the innocent by-stander, Nick asked, "Have you..."

"Have I what? I just got here. I just got out of the car. I'm lucky I made it here, you know what

I'm sayin'? I mean, it's a maze in here? Feels like I've been walking for hours."

Where's Mr. Rip..."

"Walter? He's parking the car. We got a rental. Nice folks there. Hey, if you need a rental let me know. Walter got us a pretty good deal, you know what I'm sayin'?"

"Thank you, but..."

"Oh yeah, I forgot I was talkin' to Mr. Big Shot," she nudged him with her elbow. "Probably don't have to worry 'bout rentals, do you?" She tucked her hair behind her ear mindlessly and shook her bangs from her eyes only for them to return to their familiar position.

"You look good, Nicky," she patted him again, "You look good."

Walter came in through the door and distracted her. He wore khaki slacks and a simple plaid button-down. His thinning hair was combed neatly to the side and his glasses had to stay askew on his face because he struggled with the three tote bags he'd been put in charge of.

"Well, there you are. I didn't think it was going to take you so long. Did you get lost?"

"No, I..."

"I know, these signs in here are terrible. Why'd you bring in my overnight bag?"

"I thought you said..."

"No... no..." she looked back at Nick and the girls shaking her head, "What I said was get my overnight bag out so it would be easy to find when we get to the hotel. See? See?" she turned back to

Nick again, "He just doesn't hear me." She shrugged her shoulders.

Nick smiled warmly and extended his hand. "Mr. Ripke, it's so nice to see you."

"You as well," Walter managed to say before...

"Doesn't he look good? Can you believe we've known him since he was a teen?" She looked back over her shoulder at the girls. "Time flies... and now he's a television star." She shook her head, reveling in the acquaintance. "I always knew you'd make something of yourself. I knew it."

"How was the flight?" Nick asked.

Walter intended to answer since the question was directed at him, but just didn't get the opportunity as Helen responded for him...

"Oh, don't even get me started... the food? Awful..."

Walter pushed on past her rant and addressed Nick. "We sure were sorry to hear about your parents. They were such nice people."

"Thank you. They were. I still miss..."

"Oh yeah, that's right. Car wreck, right? Some girl hit 'em head on, that's right, right?"

Nick swallowed uncomfortably and turned back to his fiancée offering his sincerest silent apologies.

"Our daughter, Bailey, got into a car wreck," she pushed on oblivious to the tension she created. "Didn't die, obviously, but do you know how much her insurance went up because of that one fender-bender? And technically it wasn't even her fault because the guy stopped in front of her, but they're going to claim it's her fault cause she's the one who hit the guy. Can you believe that? Raised her insurance by..."

"Evelynn...? Evelynn St. Lawrence?" A woman in light blue scrubs read from a clip board and scanned the room.

Evelynn caught her breath and touched each of her friends before raising her hand and breaking away from the small group.

The nurse met her half way and addressed Evelynn. "Ms. Lawrence, my name is Josey and I'll be Mr. Ripke's night nurse and I just wanted... "

"Ripke? Dave Ripke?" Helen closed the gap, "That's my son."

Josey looked uncomfortably between the two women.

Suddenly, feeling threatened, Helen looked at this other woman and snarled at her, "Who are you?"

Nick stepped between them and held up a forgiving hand to the nurse that also begged just a couple of seconds to deal with the conflict. "I'm sorry, Josey, they just arrived. Mr. and Mrs. Ripke, this is Evelynn St. Lawrence, Dave's fiancée." He took a step back and put his arm around Gwen pulling her close to him, and this... this is Guinevere, *my* fiancée."

"Isn't she the one that... *you're going to marry her*?"

"Helen, please..." Mr. Ripke interrupted. He turned his attentions toward the nurse. "I'm sorry,

Josey, is it? *We* are David's parents, could you... please, you were saying?"

Josey nodded at the man and nervously looked back down to her clip board, scanning the documents before continuing. "Umm, firstly, he is stable. I know it was touch and go there for a bit, so thank you for your patience." She looked back down searching for the next bit of information she could share. "The results of Mr. Ripke's CT scan and MRI show us that he received a blow to the back of the head here." She pointed with her pen on the human figure drawing on her paper. "Here." She turned slightly tipping her ponytail out of the way and placed her hands just below the occipital bone at the back of her skull. "There's quite a bit of intracranial pressure which causes the edema..."

"So what the hell does that mean. I'm not a doctor."

"Honey, it means that his brain is swelling..."

"How do you know?" Helen snapped at her husband. "You a doctor all of a sudden?"

"Your husband is actually correct, Mrs. Ripke." Josey pressed on; her thick southern accent trying to speak calmly.

"Well, how was I supposed to know. Why you gotta use all those fancy terms anyway. Just tell us what's going on, you know what I'm sayin'? Keep it simple."

Josey nodded, acknowledging Helen's request. "He is currently on oxygen and pain medications. If you'd like to see the list, I can get you a copy."

"Well, yeah..." Helen said sarcastically.

Josey nodded again making a note on his chart. "The doctor is administering some different medications to try and reduce the swelling. We will need to take another MRI after this round of treatment to see how he is responding and we are hoping that there is a reduction in the swelling. The MRI will also help us to make sure there are no bone fragments that may have gotten embedded in his brain."

"Can we see him?" Evelynn asked meekly. She was tired and just wanted to see him for herself.

"He is unconscious and in the critical care unit. Once we feel he is out of immediate danger, we can move him to the intensive care unit. There, you'll be able to see him one at a time, in short intervals."

Evelynn reached out and touched Josey's arm. "Thank you. Thank you for letting us know."

"Yeah, thanks. Doesn't give us much to go on..." Helen added sarcastically.

"I'm sorry, I wish I had more information for you, but for now, we just need to see if the medication will work. I'll be here all night, so I'll be back if I learn anything new or if anything changes." She placed her hand on top of Evelynn's "We're doing the best we can. He's in good hands."

Evelynn nodded and blinked, trying to keep the tears from slipping from her eyes.

Josey smiled politely at the group and exited the room.

Gwen hugged Evelynn and Nick followed suit.

Helen chuffed, "What about me? I'm his mother for crying out loud."

Evelynn straightened her shoulders and wiped her eyes. She broke away from the protective arms of her people and held a hand out to her future mother-in-law. "Mrs. Ripke, Mr. Ripke. It's a pleasure to finally meet you. Dave has told me so much about you."

Helen limply accepted her hand but said, "Yeah, well, he hasn't told us much about you, but that's Davy for ya..."

Walter crossed in front of his wife and opened his arms, "May I?"

Evelynn nodded and stepped into the embrace. "I am so glad our son found someone who makes him so happy. Welcome to the fam..."

Helen interrupted the tender moment and turned her attentions to Nick, "So, Nicky, what the hell happened out there?"

Nick began the story that brought them all to this room... Eight hours earlier...

"Hey, you guys want something to drink? I got some Pepsi... some waters... a couple of Wild Cherry Pepsi, which are for me so forget I said that... aaaand, some of this zero calorie flavored water stuff that Evie made me bring." Dave swirled his hand around the iced beverages in the under-the-seat cooler.

"I'll take a water," Nick called out, lounging on the back bench at the rear of the cruiser. Dave tossed him a plastic water bottle.

"James? Anything?"

"Nah, I'm good for now. It feels so great to just be out here, man. Thanks for the invite."

"Yeah, 'course, anytime. I'm finally starting to get the hang of her, so I'm a lil more comfortable having people on board, ya know?"

James nodded in understanding. "There's a lot to learn."

"Don't let him fool ya. He's got post-it notes all over the place to remind him of everything."

Dave laughed, "Ya had to blow my image, didn't you?" He put the lid down on the cooler and sat on the bench folding his leg across the other. "So, you moved here to be with your daughter?" Dave asked James casually.

The boat rocked gently at anchor. A sand bar was only a few feet away if they decided to swim. The river was wide at this juncture and a popular stopping point for boats before it opened up into an expansive lake.

"I'm actually from here. Born and raised, if you can believe that."

"Same." Nick chuffed. "Small world."

James nodded and smiled, "I remember you. You were a senior and I was a freshman. Just a redneck motorhead."

"Well, I was a theatre geek, so... our worlds probably wouldn't have crossed even if we were in the same grade," Nick laughed.

Dave asked James, "So small town boy seeks out big city life?" He raised his hand as if he were announcing it for a movie headline.

James grimaced, "Let's just say, I made a lot of bad choices and was hiding out from a few more. But by the grace of God, I was given a second chance. So... I've built this amazing relationship with my daughter, Danni, and I try to live every day with gratitude." He shook his head, "Cause I sure didn't deserve that second chance."

Nick stood and leaned forward, extending his hand to James who was leaning against the Captain's chair. "Amen to that brother," he put his other hand over their clasped hands. "None of us deserves His grace, but He must see something worthy..." Nick laughed good-naturedly.

"Seriously?" Helen's rasping voice pulled Nick back from his story. "You gonna tell us what you had for lunch too?" She threw up her hands and let them fall to her sides. "No offense, Nicky, I mean, you spin a great yarn and all, but I didn't fly all this way to hear about your relaxing day on the water while my son is in there fighting for his life: and I don't get to go in there and see him and find out these answers for myself."

"It was my fault."

The room fell silent as everyone turned to see who the voice belonged to.

Gwen crossed the room to hug them. "James." She cautiously embraced him over his hospital gown, wires and tubes and I.V. pole. "Nina." She turned and hugged her too, motioning them to come in and sit. "Are you alright?"

He nodded as he moved gingerly, allowing his right leg to carry most of the weight, while Nina followed closely behind pushing the I.V. pole. He sat on the edge of one of the seats keeping his leg extended. His arm was loosely bandaged and hung in a sling. He shrugged off any pain he might be feeling.

Nick came over to his friend. "It's not your fault. It was an accident."

"Speak up. I can't hear you." Helen talked over everyone's low voices. "Who is this guy?" Helen asked Evelynn, making her a co-conspirator.

"James... Nina... this is Mr. and Mrs Ripke, David's parents. James was on the boat with Nick and David," Evelynn summed it up.

When James tried to face David's parents, he was filled with shame, unable to keep eye contact, so heavy was the burden he placed on himself. "Mr. Ripke. Mrs. Ripke. I am so very sorry about ..."

"What happened out there, son?" Walter sat beside him and placed a hand on his shoulder.

"We think," James looked to Nick for confirmation and got straight to the meat of the situation, "that fumes built up in the motor. Either the blower wasn't on or it wasn't on long enough before we turned over the engine." James rubbed his forehead and shook his head trying to remember.

"This causes the fumes to build up..." Nick added.

"If I would have just opened the fuel tank or checked the blower..."

Nina stroked his back supporting him through this confession.

"Before we knew what happened..." James continued, sighing heavily, "... he turned the key and cranked the motor, it exploded. The whole thing... it just..."

Nick picked up where James left off. "The cover hit David throwing him from the boat seconds before the explosion. He hit his head going over the side. When the motor caught fire, that's what caused the burns to James' arm and leg as he was thrown from the boat. Basically, Dave being thrown from the boat may have saved his life."

"Well, we don't know that, yet, now do we?" Helen snapped.

James shook his head with the memory.

"The explosion could have done so much more damage to you, James. You're so lucky." Gwen offered.

"I don't feel lucky."

"Pffft." Helen rolled her eyes. "At least he's out walking around."

"Helen," Walter admonished.

"Mrs. Ripke, Nick here saved your son's life." James ignored her prior comment. "In that split second before the motor caught fire..." he paused to shake his head again. "Dave was already unconscious when he hit the water. He would have drowned if Nick hadn't dove in to save him."

Evelynn, who had been quietly listening from a distance having heard bits of the story earlier came forward. "Is that true?" She stood in front of Nick.

"It's not that big..."

"Is it true?" she asked again.

He shrugged, suddenly self-conscious. "It's true. He's my best friend. I wasn't trying to be heroic or anything... it just... I acted on instinct..."

Evelynn moved closer and wrapped her arms around his waist laying her head on his chest. "Thank you," she spoke barely above a whisper.

"I love him too, Evie," Nick whispered softly as he returned the embrace.

Chapter Eleven

"Thank you all for coming tonight. And Gill, thank you again and again for feeding us all in the waiting room, all week."

The small classroom was filled with staff, cast of the upcoming show and supporters for an impromptu meeting called by Evelynn and Guinevere. Everyone clapped softly for Gillian's generosity.

Gill smiled and shrugged her shoulders, "If you're already cooking for eight, what's a few more?"

"Well it has been so appreciated."

"Yeah, one can only live on chips and Cheez-its for so long." Gwen laughed.

Evelynn took in a deep breath before she stood. She massaged the bridge of her nose and smoothed her hair back toward her dancer's bun. "Okay, so, for those of you who haven't heard, my fiancé, David Ripke- you've seen him around here with the camera on his shoulder was in a boating accident. They have tried medications to reduce the swelling in his brain but he, being his stubborn self, decided not to cooperate," she nervously laughed. "So... they are putting him in a medically induced coma." Her voice cracked and she paused to take a quick breath while the room of people waited patiently.

"They are hoping..." again her words cut off with emotion.

Gwen stood and went beside her best friend and held her hand. "From what we understand," Gwen continued, "the doctors think his body might heal better on it's own if it has time to rest. So, a medically induced coma is basically a forced resting period."

Evelynn nodded and wiped away a tear.

"Since the brain is the most complex organ, it is always running. So all of Dave's... uh... systems will be hooked up to machines, that will do the work of the brain, and he will be monitored every step of the way."

"Will he be breathing on his own?" Jenni asked.

"*All* his systems," Gwen repeated.

"What if..." the fateful question came from the back of the room.

Gwen took in a deep breath to answer it but Evelynn patted her hand.

"Dave's parents will have to make that decision of whether to keep him hooked up to the machines."

"So... his parents? They'll be staying?" Gillian asked cautiously... respectfully.

Nick stood to answer and looked over to Gillian sympathetically, "Yes, I'm afraid they will be staying."

There was a murmuring across the room and it seemed that everyone shared the same opinion.

"That woman is just plain mean," Lucas said what was on everyone's mind.

"She's always so angry..."

"Nothing is ever her fault..."

"She's always up in everyone else's business..."

"She always has an answer for everything..."

Evelynn raised her hand to quiet the small classroom. "I know that she... comes across acidic, at times..." she began.

Lucas huffed loudly.

"...but, please remember that it is her *son* hooked up to all those machines and wires. So, please, as much as it depends on you, be respectful and be at peace. Just walk away if you need to."

"Everyone handles stress and grief differently."

"Well, she handles it by giving it to everybody else," Lucas couldn't hold his tongue.

Gwen scolded him with a look.

"I know, I know... 'be nice'." He air-quoted the direct order. "But... Jesus don't like ugly."

"You just let Jesus worry about that, alright?" Gwen hoped to cut off further comments on the subject.

"How is James?" Betty asked, changing the subject.

"Danni?" Evelynn offered, "Do you want to take this one?"

"Uh yeah," Danni stood up and pulled a folded slip of paper from her front jeans pocket then unfolded it.

"Uh first, um... thank you everyone for the bouquet of flowers, but he requests that you don't send anymore. 'I'm not dead, yet'" she gave her best "dad" voice and rolled her eyes. She looked down at her paper for her next speaking point.

"The burns on his arm and sides weren't as bad and should be healing in a couple weeks. The ones on his leg might take longer 'cause some nerve damage may have happened and some scarring. But they are keeping him in the hospital for another week because he refuses to do what the nurses tell him, which is to mainly stay in bed," she shrugged her shoulders, looking around the room at everyone. "His girlfriend, Nina, uh... Miss Black is with him most evenings after school and I'm with him during the day." She turned her attention to Evelynn and Gwen, "which is why I still would like to do my part in the show. Please let me do my part. You know how I feel about hospitals in the first place and my dad said he'd rather me do it too. 'I don't need a babysitter,' he says."

Evelynn and Gwen looked at each other and smiled. Evelynn nodded and Gwen said, "Okay, the part is still yours."

Evelynn stood up again as Danni sat down smiling. "Thank you for the update, sweetie. We will definitely keep your dad in our prayers." She took in a deep breath before continuing. "And since Danni brought it up, we need to make a few changes. Opening night is tomorrow, and this is going to sound terrible," Evelynn shook her head, "but the doctors agreed to hold off the procedure until we close the opening weekend shows on Sunday, so I can be there..." she swallowed hard, "... just in case.. it doesn't..." She cleared her throat but the sentence didn't really need finishing. "For the remainder of the run, Diana is going to step into my roll as Dolly and Jenni is going to take over her role in the chorus."

"We're going to have to let out her costumes a little," Jenni giggled, lightening the mood.

"I have no boobs, I'm sorry!" Diana teased.

"And I have plenty to spare!" Jenni laughed.

"How 'bout we meet in the middle. We'll let out your costumes for Jenni and pad you up for mine," Evelynn teased. It felt good to laugh with her people.

Her people... they were all here because they loved her, loved Dave and loved the theatre and would do what needed to be done. And it was because of these people that she knew she could step away and take care of things.

"Everything else will continue as planned. The show will run its scheduled dates, which will bring us up to the weekend prior to Thanksgiving. There will be no hold-overs."

Evelynn's eyes burned as a sheen clouded her vision. Her throat constricted and felt like it was getting tighter, no matter how many times she swallowed. The room was respectfully silent seeing her try to carry on.

"And... as you know..." she gulped. "... that next weekend was scheduled to be... our...

wedding." A tear slipped down her cheek as her voice cracked, forcing the words to come out.

Gwen attempted to come to her side again, but Evelynn held her in place by raising her hand.

"I would like... we would like... Nick and Gwen to get married in our place."

"Noooo..." Gwen shook her head and spoke out over the murmurs in the room. Tears poured from both the best friends' eyes.

Evelynn raised her hand again to silence the room.

"Hear me out," Evelynn pleaded, "... just...hear me out... please."

The room quieted again and Nick held Gwen's hand.

"You have been so generous waiting for Dave and I to have our day. You kept your engagement low key, so it wouldn't take away from my shine, you were patient as we moved the December date back into November, you made that beautiful dress for me... and you have both stood by us and helped us plan our day and pretended to be as excited as if it were your own..." she swallowed air unable to keep her tears in check any longer. "And now..." she gulped, "... our day is being... postponed... until ... further notice..." she paused to collect herself and wipe away the tears on her face. "It's not fair to expect you to keep on waiting for a day... that we don't know if..."

"Evie..." Gwen attempted, but couldn't speak either.

Evelynn shook off her emotions and squared off her shoulders, tired of blubbering... "It's not fair for you to put off your life together and put everything on hold because my boyfriend forgot how to drive a boat." Her attempt at humor fell flat as everyone in the room felt the weight of her grief and the generosity of her gift.

"And you already love the dress..." Evelynn's tears found their way back out again. "And it would fit you beautifully..." Her words were a series of high-pitched squeaks by now. "And we've already paid for the cake..." she broke down and was instantly swarmed with arms of love to support her. She and Gwen stood forehead to forehead crying as the room gathered their strength around them.

But now... it had been spoken... and all of the theatre family mourned with each other.

Chapter Twelve

"Okay, this week I found some devotionals that I've been wanting to do but never found the time. So, thanks, honey, now I have plenty of time, plus I thought you might need a break from me reading scripts. I know I do." Evelynn laughed.

"You doin' okay?" she asked pausing as if there would be a reply as she rifled through her stack of books. "It looks like you need a shave again. I'd better do that before your mom gets here. But if it's not the shave, it will be something else, I'm sure. I'm trying to love her, I really am, but she sure doesn't make it easy." She fluffed his pillows, just to be doing something before sitting down and getting comfortable. "And you didn't even warn me! Unforgivable." She stroked his scruffly cheek with her thumb. "Okay... fine... I forgive you." She pushed his bangs away from his face. "I'll keep trying. I can see that she loves you, in her way; that she's worried about you... I'm sure there's that warm squishy spot in there somewhere... Your father must see it too... The most patient man I've ever met, I think. I like him a lot," she smiled as she spoke.

She needlessly smoothed out his sheets and rested her hand on his leg to make sure the circulation leg wraps were working properly. She only had to wait a few moments before the wrap vibrated under her hand, massaging his leg muscles so atrophy doesn't set in and blood clots don't form. Not realizing that she was holding her breath while waiting, she knows that she can't control certain things, but she released her breath as the motorized wrap did it's job. She mentally scolded herself. She has to let go and trust that the doctors and nurses are doing their very best.

She looked up at his face. It looked so calm. So serene. But she knew that just underneath the thin layer of blankets, was an entire hidden blueprint of wires and tubes all working together in some scientific way to save this man's life. Does he know what is happening to him? Does he know that he is dancing on the edge of life and death? Evelynn shuddered.

She moved up the bed and stroked his face once again. "Are you in there my love? Can you hear me? Are you ready to come back to me?" She sat in the chair beside his bed and took his hand in hers. "I am missing you terribly. I know, that on the outside, it doesn't seem like we fit together. To be honest... I've doubted it a time or two myself. But... I know... I know that you're the one for me... and ... if you leave me now, after it taking so long to find you... I... I may never recover. I settled for what I thought could be love... someday. If I loved enough for us both, he would eventually love me. But I can see... feel the difference with you. You show me what love really is. You show me what it feels like to be cared for, respected... liked." She shrugged at the simplicity of it all. She took in a deep breath and pushed it out. "So..." she concluded, "if you're planning on leaving me, you might as well make space for me in heaven with you and we'll just get married there. That's right. You're not getting away that easy, sir" She paused and stroked his hand with her thumb. "But... if you need more time to rest, I'll be here... waiting for you... boring you to death with scripts and devotionals." She leaned back and thought for a moment. "Maybe I can go buy one of those motorcycle magazines you like to look at and read to you from that. Are there even any articles in those?" She sat there for a moment holding his hand, sitting in silence pretending it was just another Tuesday afternoon...

She sat up and released his hand releasing a heavy sigh, "But, until then... I got this series that Gillian recommended. *Leading with Love*. We can work on those." She opened the book, settled back, grabbed his hand again and began reading.

"Why is it so hot in here? Are you kidding me? Don't we pay enough to get a little A.C. in this place?" Helen leaned back out the doorway and yelled toward the nurse's station. "Hey! Could we get a fan in here or something? It's stuffy." She came further into the room and set her bags down. "Can't we just get some air circulating in here, or something? You know what I'm sayin'?"

Evelynn stood in front of her chair and set the book down. She clasped Dave's hand with both of hers and in her cheeriest expression she said, "Hello, M... M.... uh.... Mom..."

Helen froze in her tracks and Evelynn regretted her attempts. The silence carried for only a few seconds, but for Evelynn, it felt like hours.

"You been here all morning?"

Evelynn nodded, no longer trusting her words.

"Has it been this hot in here the whole time?

Evelynn shook her head, "I... it seems... fine... I..."

Helen pointed her finger at Evelynn, "Well, that's how infection spreads, I guarantee it," she huffed.

Helen walked to the foot of the bed and lay her hand on his covered feet and stared quietly at her son. She watched his chest rise and fall in a rhythmic pattern. To the unsuspecting eye, he was merely sleeping. No one from the outside could see the battle that he was fighting underneath his calm repose.

"Huh," she huffed out and patted his foot gently.

Evelynn looked on at the moment of gentleness, her heart filling with hope.

"Who do I have to sleep with around here to get my son clean shaven?

Evelynn was visibly shocked by her abrasive words.

Helen laughed and shook her head at the stupidity of the world and more poignantly, the lack of quality service in this particular establishment. "You know what I'm sayin'? They're just sittin' out there. This place is a dump. We need to get you outa here, boy."

Evelynn swallowed hard, but stayed quiet.

Helen finally looked at Evelynn as if she just now noticed her. "You leavin'?"

"Well, I was..." she nodded back to her book.

"Why don't you go ahead and stay a while. I brought us some donuts. She leaned down for one of her bags and forced the box from the confines of the plastic grocery bag. She set the box on Dave's legs. After catching Evelynn's look, she muttered, "He ain't gonna care," she jerked her thumb in his direction. "Have you seen him eat?" She lifted the lid enticingly, almost demanding that Evelynn take one. And just at that moment, the circulation wraps turned on, vibrating the donut box. "Ha, look," Helen said amused, "Now they're dancing donuts. You should like those, right? You're a dancer or something, right? Go ahead, help yourself."

She glanced up at Dave's expressionless face in either apology or permission and took an iced cake donut. She uncomfortably sat back down.

"I guess I have to go down to the 'guest room', she air-quoted, "to get me some coffee. Don't know why I bother, it's gonna taste like crap, you know what I'm sayin'?"

She pulled the reclining chair closer to the opposite side of Dave's bed and plugged her phone and charger into the outlet of the wall.

"Well, here goes nothin'. I'll be back. Take you another donut," and she exited the room.

Evelynn waited until she was around the corner before addressing her fiancé, "Honey, I hope nothing happens to your father, because your mom is going to have to go to a nursing home. Please don't let her have to stay with us." She looked down... she looked around the room guiltily, while she held herself, biting her lip. She breathed out heavily. "I'm sorry, I shouldn't have said that. I hope you didn't hear any of that." She leaned over the side of the bed to kiss Dave's forehead. She ran her hand over the stubbles on his cheek. "I love your scruffy face."

"Oh Rip, man... I wish you could have been there. I mean, not only because you're the best camera man around, but it just doesn't feel the same without you." Nick came into the room and moved the arm chair back over next to the bed. "It was so great being out with the people again. And what a turn out! There were so... so many volunteers. Okay, sure, there were a few lookers, and autograph seekers, but honestly, these were real people sincerely looking for an outlet to help: Get their hands dirty helping others. Immediate results. It was great, man. We had plenty of tools, and supplies... and food! Dude, you would have been in heaven, there was so much food!

"I got to interview about a dozen workers. I wish there was time for more, but putting a week's worth of work into an hour long episode is tough. I'm going to take on the editing for these first couple episodes to see if it's going to fly, and then we'll see if we can hire out... or maybe get a volunteer for that too?" he shrugged, "I dunno. Anything is possible, I guess.

"So yeah, we got six houses almost done. Some finishing work still has to be done, but we can get to that without the cameras. Six. Not bad. We were shooting for eight, but I can be happy with six. I still have to fill in some dialogue, but I can practically do that in my sleep.

"Oh, and Monica Kelley showed up to the worksite with her camera crew. She promised to give us some airtime. I'm so jazzed about this... the *Phoenix Project*. Has a nice ring to it, huh?"

He slapped his thighs, "Man, it felt so good to be back doin' what I do... but this time, making a difference." His voice cracked and he swallowed the lump in his throat. "You're a part of that, buddy.   The *Phoenix Project* wouldn't have happened without....you... and Gwen."   He swallowed again and rubbed the sweat from his palms on his thighs.

He looked at his hands as he attempted to continue, "Gwen and I... we're supposed to be deciding if we want to get married on your day." He paused letting those words settle into the air.

"This isn't a decision we're taking lightly. I want you to know that. If... if we choose to do it, it would be to honor you. Not take anything away from you, of course." He wrung his hands, continuing, "But, I'm going to be honest with you, I am having trouble seeing myself making the most important decision in my life without my best friend there beside me. I just... I can't see it, you know?"

He rested his elbows on his knees threading and unthreading his fingers. "We tossed around a few ideas, like us getting married at the same time, you know, when you're feeling better... but we just don't know when, or..." he let his words drop not wanting to complete the sentence.

"We... uh... we thought about just going to the Justice of the Peace and then waiting to have a wedding later, after you guys....

"Or... or... we could just wait... I guess... I want to be married but I don't want to... oh," he dropped his head and ran his fingers through his hair." "This sucks, man."

He paused and the corners of his mouth lifted. He sat up and nudged the bed, "Maybe, we'll just perform the ceremony here. You'll wake up and you'll already be married." He laughed. "I know how much you hate tuxes," he laughed again. "You're welcome."

He nodded for no particular reason and scanned the room for no particular thing.

"I miss you, man. I'm... so sorry this happened. I... I should have... been paying more attention. I knew better. Stupid mistake. I could have... should have..." he swallowed, overwhelmed. "Bud, I need you to come out of this. I am so sorry."

"Oh honey, *Annie Get Your Gun* has been a huge success! We have sell-out shows for almost the entire run! Our opening weekend got great reviews and it ended up being standing room only!" The audiences have been amazing, the cast has said. Very responsive, great applause, laughing... Oh, honey, it just makes my heart so happy! I won't bore you with numbers, but we just... oh... we just have such a great cast!" Evelynn was excitedly pacing around the room removing her gloves and coat and scarf.

"I don't know if you remember Diana, she's such a tiny, petite thing. Light skinned and the perfect dancer's body, although she says she's not interested in dancing... but hold that thought," Evelynn laughed at her powers of persuasion when it came to actors realizing their hidden talents, "but her voice! It just blew everyone away!"

She stopped at the end of the bed and continued as if she had an interactive partner. "And the kids! The kids are doing such a great job!

They are doing the intermission entertainment now too, Gwen said. I know you can't see it, but here," she walked over to her bag and pulled out stacks of colored paper, "These... these are all from the kids." She set the stack on his bedside table and opened a couple of the cards to set them up. She wiped a tear from her cheek. "Cards... and pictures... they all made you something. How sweet is that? They ask me about you every time they see me. Oh honey, you are so missed."

"Hello son," Walter spoke from the door before entering. "Your mother is off grocery shopping and getting her hair done and some other such things. She needs some pampering. She's under a lot of stress, so she tells me." He laughed to himself. He cautiously walked into the room waiting for someone to tell him that he didn't belong there and should leave. But no one did. So he approached the bed. I... I thought I'd come by and have some time with you, myself. You know when your mother takes over, it's just better to get out of the way." He laughed nervously and looked around the room to confirm that he was alone. "I'm sorry for not being here as much as I'd like... but... I am here now."

"Your bride to be is spending the day at the uh… the theatre. She said she had some office work she could catch up on so I could be here with you… She's a great gal, your Evie. I like her a lot. She's a hard worker. And she… cares about you a lot. That's obvious. She's practically put her whole world on hold to be here with you as much as possible."

He cleared his throat searching for things to say. He moved around the room looking and listening to all the foreign items attached to his only son.

"Not much has changed in real estate… although the internet, I'll say, has really helped." He turned and smiled at his son and realized again that this conversation was one-sided. "It uh… I don't have to leave my office nearly as much as I used to. And I have even been able to work on a few deals while I've been here. Which is good. Keeps me busy." He pulled the heavy curtain back a few inches to look out over the rooftop of the other half of the sprawling hospital. The trees were stripped of their leaves and the only color was the occasional spruce or the neatly trimmed shrubbery that lined the entranceway. He looked out at nothing for a few moment before speaking again.

"You know your mother… she means well. She wasn't always this way." He slipped his hands into the pockets of his navy blue slacks and wandered away from the window. "She was once full of vim and vigor… full of life," he smiled at the memory. "You know we met at the same church camp that we sent you to." He leaned against the glass wall at the foot of the bed. "I thought she was the most beautiful girl I'd ever seen.

"Oh, I knew even then, she was too much for me to handle, but, oh how I loved that spark in her." He folded his arms across his chest, remembering. "She had the world at her feet and she was going to bend it to her will and teach it a thing or two along the way. Such dreams, such... passion."

He shrugged away those yesterdays, "But then, things happen. Life happened. She was dealt a series of blows... and ... I just don't think she was able to recover from them. Maybe not even today. I know she has pushed you and your sister away and I'm sorry for that. I don't think she even realizes she's doing it.

"I'm not making excuses for her... or... maybe I am. I just... I don't know... I am hoping, while you're in there... thinking your thoughts that maybe you could remember her how she used to be.

"She loves you, son. She does. I know at times she made it easy for you to walk away and I know that you have tried to mend fences, and..." he sighed.

"Whatever happens, I hope you know that she... and I... love you."

Evelynn read out loud from the devotional and Helen sat on the other side playing a game on her phone. It had become their daily routine. The high-pitched artificial music telling all in the room of Helen's success or failure at the game was always in direct conflict with the steady rhythmic beeping of the machines keeping David's artificial life functioning.

Evelynn stayed quiet as Helen unleashed her anger on anyone or anything around her.

"This stupid game. I swear it cheats. It wants me to pay for the upgraded version... I'm not doing that." She tapped a few more buttons and the music responded. "See? See what I mean? It gets you used to playing one way and now they're gonna add grapes? Seriously?"

Evelynn, who doesn't speak the language of phone games offered, "Maybe it's trying to increase your dexterity."

Helen stared at her blankly. "Whatever. They just want my money. It's only a buck ninety-nine, but still..."

Evelynn nodded her head in understanding of the evils of the game creators. She went back to reading out loud to the still silent David Ripke.

"Do you really think he can hear you?"

Evelynn paused again and looked at Helen, contemplating her answer. She furrowed her brow slightly thinking, "I hope so. I hope he knows that we are here for him and that he's not fighting all alone."

"He probably doesn't even know he's fighting."

Evelynn looked back down at her book.

"That stuff you're reading, bout being patient and not judging others, my daughter needs to hear that. She's got a mouth on her. Doesn't appreciate anything anyone does for her. Yeah, she needs to hear that stuff. Maybe I'll get her that book. Not that she'll read it. Can't make that girl do anything."

Evelynn bit her tongue knowing that this woman is completely oblivious to the comparisons she is making. She didn't need any encouragement to continue her conversation.

"Do you know how much money I have spent on her and those kids? Her lazy husband won't get a job. Hell, I've paid their rent for the last three months. Three months? What happened to the time when a man would feel shame for not supporting his family? He don't care." She was talking while playing her game mindlessly. "Do you think I get any 'gratitude'" she air-quoted the word and rolled her eyes.

Helen stared at Evelynn, finally requiring some participation. Evelynn smiled and silently prayed for the right words.

"Maybe," she began, "... maybe your daughter isn't around people who speak kindly? Sometimes we mirror what we are most exposed to."

"You got that right. That whole 'birds of a feather' thing. Yeah, I heard you reading about that earlier.   Her husband, "she rolled her eyes again, "There's a piece of work, I tell ya."

She paused her game and let the lower half of the chair down on the recliner in order to face her.

Evelynn's stomach knotted, knowing there was about to be a toxic rant coming and she had no place to run and no authority to silence it.

"Did you know her husband wouldn't let her come here to be with her brother? Her only brother. You know what I'm sayin'? I wouldn't put up with that, I tell ya. I mean, if her brother dies..."

"Please don't say that."

"...I hope she feels guilty. I hope she does. It'll serve her right."

Evelynn prayed hard, hoping that her fiancé couldn't hear these words.   "We don't know everything about her situation. She might..."

"Oh yes we do. She's just selfish. If it's not about her or if she doesn't get her way... she's a..." Helen paused. "Well, I won't say it cause I know you're not a cussing person... but she's the 'b-word'. You know what I'm sayin'? Sad I have to say that about my own daughter, but, there ya go. She'll get what's comin' to her."

She leaned back thinking she was out of words, but then remembered, "You know I even tried to get her to go to church?" She swatted the air, "Whatever."

Evelynn took in a deep breath before saying, "People don't change until they see a *need* to change."

Evelynn hoped that the deeper meaning of her words left their mark on her future mother-in-laws heart, but knew they fell on deaf ears when she replied, "You got that right. She ain't gonna change. She's as stubborn as they come."

Helen looked over at her sleeping son and her face softened. "My Davey now,... not a mean bone in his body."

Evelynn smiled at her words, knowing they were true.

"He may not be the brightest crayon in the box, you know what I'm sayin'? But that boy has got a good heart."

Evelynn reached out to touch Dave's hand thankful that the conversation shifted.

"He had to go to summer school two summers. Know what I mean?" She tapped her head, "Not too smart. But he doesn't give up. He just keeps coming back for more." She shook her head. "I like you," she mentioned as she gathered up her things. "I think you'll be good for him and Lord knows, he's crazy about you. Didn't tell me much, for whatever reason, I'm only his mother, you know what I'm sayin'? But his dad... he went on and on about you to Walter."

Helen did everything she could not to make eye contact, but instead kept her hands busy. "Davy is just like his dad. He won't let go. Sees the good in people." She raised her eyes to Evelynn and she could see a sheen over them. "You could treat him like garbage, but he won't let go. He'll just take it. I don't believe you got it in you to do that to him and I hope that never changes. I gotta get outta here. See you around."

And with that, she picked up her several bags and walked out through the sliding glass door.

Evelynn was speechless and couldn't move or even blink for a moment. But it was only a second before Helen popped back in through the door.

"You can call me Mom if you want to." And she was gone again.

Evelynn's eyes welled up with tears and a giggle escaped. "Thank you," she whispered quietly to the room. "Thank you."

Gwen and Nick walked through the heavy solid door to the Intensive care unit of the hospital and heard their own voices reverberate down the hallway.

Confused, they looked at each other and kept walking toward the source, which was Dave's room.

His glass door was held open and Nick and Gwen's version of the fictional opera *Czaritza* based on *Tchaikovsky's Fifth Symphony* was being piped into the halls from a speaker next to Dave's bed.

The nurse stopped in her tracks when she rounded the corner and almost crashed into the real live performers of the music playing overhead.

"Oh! Oh my gosh! It's you!" she gushed. "I... uh... I hope you don't mind..."

Gwen and Nick looked at each other again, obviously confused. "What's going on?"

"Oh you're mad... I can... It's totally my fault," the young nurse admitted. "Miss Evelynn turned this CD on for Mr. Ripke last night and we all fell in love with it. We decided to share it with the other patients. The whole collection is so beautiful and SUCH a nice break from the Muzack, and it's so soothing we thought..." she rattled on as fast as the words could escape her mouth.

"Thank you, but..." Nick began.

"...those songs are no where near professional quality." Gwen continued.

"We just threw them together for Rip... uh... Mr. Ripke."

The nurse covered her heart with her hands, "Oh, we just love them. Could we... would you mind if we keep playing them?"

"But they're not very good. We literally... I mean, we barely practiced, before we..."

"My mom is a big fan of Jeanette MacDonald and Nelson Eddy and I can tell you must be too."

Nick offered, "My mom too. We had a steady influence of MacEddy growing up"

The nurse smiled. "Us too. Reminds me of her when I hear those songs." She turned to Gwen, "and they sound great." Gwen cringed as she spoke. "And we didn't hear anything you should feel upset about. We... the other nurses and I really think it helps the patients. Many of them seem to be responding."

"Yeah, probably inwardly begging you to turn it off," Gwen furrowed her brows.

Nick nudged her and continued speaking to the nurse. "How's it doing for our guy?" Nick asked.

"Well, unfortunately," the nurse offered, "Mr. Ripke's systems are all being controlled and adjusted by the doctors, so all of our readings for him are... doctor made... so to speak."

"Oh," Nick looked disappointed.

She reached out and touched them both on their arms. "I do believe he can hear you reaching out to him. We don't know if everything registers, but music is so deeply ingrained in our brains, that it is one of the best ways to reach our people, while they are healing from surgery or recuperating from an extensive injury or," she smiled, "for when a patient is healing from a coma."

Gwen smiled. "Thank you for that. It's so hard to stay positive sometimes when there are no visible changes."

The nurse nodded in understanding. "Well, as of the last CT scan, it looks like there has been some reduction in the swelling. The doctors are pleased with his progress so far. So keep doing what you're doing. It seems to be working."

"Yeah, I guess that goes for you guys too," Nick laughed.

"Okay Buddy, you're getting awfully close to the deadline here. You need to quit goofing off and wake up now. There are people who still need you. Me included.

"I know how you love being the center of attention so I've got all the pastors coming out after church on Sunday to do a laying on of hands. And I need you on board with it. Do you hear me?"

Nick stood up alongside his friend and placed a hand on his shoulder and held Dave's limp hand with the other. "Do you hear me, brother? I need you to fight. Don't let go, man. It's not time."

He wiped away tears with his elbow so as not to break their physical connection. "I mean it. If you leave me, I'm going to make up the lamest way you could have possibly died."

He paused thinking.

"...attacked by kittens... fishing naked..." He searched his brain for another example, "... allergic reaction to... to... chocolate... I don't know, dude. Don't make me have to do it."

Nick moved to sit at the edge of the bed. "But since you are here and you're sort of a captive audience..." Nick looked around guiltily rubbing the back of his neck. "You remember that time you got drunk in college and I told you that you ate all the Oreo cookies? Well, that was me. I was so mad that you got wasted, I figured that you didn't deserve the cookies, so I ate them. All of them." He looked down again, "If it makes you feel any better, they made me sick.

"And... I mean, since we're being honest here... You remember that time at camp when that kid Billy Croop who wanted to beat you up because you accidently tripped over his shoe and made him drop his marshmallow in the fire... That whole... 'meet-you-at-midnight-thing'...I... I... might have accidentally threatened his life if he didn't apologize and call the whole thing off." Nick looked off into the distance at nothing before deciding to defend himself to his comatose friend. "I knew he could really do some damage and I knew that you would go through with it because Tiffany Schriever was there and you would have done anything to get her attention. ... even if it was stupid. Yeah... so there was that..."

Nick stood and paced at the foot of the bed. "Whoo! That's a load off my mind. I've been carrying that around for years." He paced back and forth a few more times clenching and unclenching his fist. "Okay, fine... there's one more thing. Freshman year... college. That girl...

Sylvia... SSSS sssomething... she was only flirting with you because she was trying to get back at me. She wanted me to go out with her and when I said 'no', she started flirting with you whenever I was around.... So... I made up the story that she was cheating with you on her boyfriend in Germany. I knew that you wouldn't want to go out with her because... well, integrity... you have it..." He raised his arms up and let them flop at his sides. He said his confession so fast that he used up his entire breath to utter them.

He went back to the arm chair and sat down. "We've been friends for a long time, Rip. Long... long time. We've been through a lot. Seen a lot. You've always been there for me, long before I ever had money, and your friendship hasn't changed since I've become successful. Good friends are hard to find, much less keep." He leaned forward placing his elbows on his knees. "It takes a lot of seasons, good and bad to make a friendship that lasts a lifetime."

He laughed as his eyes teared up with emotion, "I need to write this down, it'd be great for my best man speech at your wedding."

He stood up and pinched the bridge of his nose. "I gotta go; a few more shows in the run. And... just to let you know... Gwen and I decided to wait to get married. I need my best man. So use this time to work on your best man speech. And, you can't use the stuff I came up with either."

He patted Dave's arm, "So... your wedding date is still available if you want to perform any miracles or anything."

He moved away to leave but came back to the bed once more and leaned down close to Dave's ear. "I know you're going to come out of this, brother. I just know it. God's got plans for you, yet."

"...and if you follow these eleven tips, your boss will know that you are taking your job seriously and are ready to take it to the next level." Evelynn read from the October issue of GQ magazine.

"Okay, now that we know what socks to wear, which watch means business and a few new office tips... let's see what's next." Evelynn flipped through the pages and pages of ads. "Nope, you'll never wear this." Flip, flip... "Why would *anyone* wear this?" Flip... flip... "Okay, here's something..." she began to read. "Is your relationship Hot Stuff or Cold Fish? What?" She re-read the title making sure she saw it correctly. She looked around the room to make sure she was alone before reading more. "It's a quiz." She folded the one side of the magazine back. "Should we?" She giggled to herself. She looked around the room again, and pushed a cheek full of air out... "Let's do it."

"Question one. Do you and your partner kiss in public. PDA's? Oh... that's not so bad. Yes. Oooo! We get five points for that. Okay. Question number two. Do you think your mate is a good kisser?" she giggled and looked up at her fiancé. "Yes. Another five points. Question three. Did your parents have the 'sex talk with you or did you find out on your own?" she laughed. "Okay, am I supposed to be answering for you or for me..." she grabbed a pen from the side table, "But, I'm going to put a star by that one, cause I sure want to hear the answer! Especially now that I've met your parents! I can only *imagine* that coming from Helen or Walter." She wrote an asterisk by the question and moved on to the next one. "Question four. What's your favorite time of the day for sex... oh my...."

The doctor was satisfied with the results of the latest CT scan and decided that it was time to pull David Ripke back to the land of the living. Medication to keep Dave in his medically induced coma had been stopped and pain meds had taken its place.

The doctor pulled Evelynn and his parents to the side. "You need to prepare for the worst," he began, getting their attention. "The brain swelling *has* gone down and his vitals are looking pretty good, but he was under a little longer than we usually like to take our patients. He may take a few hours to wake up: he may not be able to speak for weeks... he may have nightmares... he may not even remember why he is here... or..." the doctor cleared his throat, "he may not wake up at all."

"What kind of chance are we looking at here, doctor?"

"I'm not going to lie, it's not looking good. It took a long time for the edema to recede, and usually when that happens, it is an indication to deeper trauma."

"Oh, but he's always been a slow healer," Helen put out there.

"I don't want to tell you it's over, but... it's now up to Mr. Ripke. If he wants to live, he's going to have to fight for it. And for every hour he stays under, the harder it's going to be to bring him back. I would... say your good-byes," the doctor looked away and shrugged, "but like I said, it's up to him."

"I'm praying for you son. You've got to pull through this."

"Rip, buddy, come on... come back to us."

"David, you've become such a part of our lives. Please, please don't give up."

"Davy, don't you dare leave me. You know I wouldn't be able to take it. I will never forgive you if you don't keep fighting."

"My David... verse three in The Song of Solomon says, 'I have found the one whom my soul loves'. This... this is you, for me. My love. My soul has been lonely for so long. Please don't make me wait to have to find you again. Come back to me. I love you..."

Come back...
Come back...
Come back...

Chapter Thirteen

Evelynn looked at herself in the mirror. Her eyes were red-rimmed and on the verge of spilling over once again, but she insisted on trying to apply make-up.

Candlelight was the only illumination in her bathroom. A glass of wine and the half empty bottle sat on the closed toilet seat-turned-table.

She had stayed strong for so long.

She pinned her hair carefully to create a waterfall of curls.

She added pearl studded earrings to match her simple, yet elegant, string of pearls necklace.

She dabbed her cheeks and under her eyes with a tissue and discarded it on the pile in the trash bin. Her beautiful reflection showed resignation... defeat... the very essence of sadness.

The silence engulfed her, almost choking her, and she did not attempt to escape it.

She stepped into her dress and slid it up and over her shoulders. Reaching behind her, she pulled the zipper closed.

She walked barefoot from the bathroom to the window in her darkened, candlelit office.

Snow. Big, white snowflakes fell from the grey sky. The first snowfall of the year.

Evelynn walked down the hall and into the dressing room and curled up onto the plush wingback chair. She couldn't stop the tears.

"This was supposed to be my wedding day."

The main door to the Centre opened and clicked closed. The time has come. They would be looking for her. They would expect her to put on a brave face for the others.. She couldn't. She just knew she couldn't.

Evelynn heard hurried footsteps in the hall. They were looking in her office now. The footsteps scurried further down the hall checking in each of the classrooms along the way. There was just one more hallway of rooms before reaching the stage entrances... the dressing rooms. Evelynn made no attempt to help the searcher to locate her.

"Evie? Gwen stuck her head in the women's dressing room and almost pulled it back out before she spotted the figure in the corner.

"Oh Evie... my poor Evie. Why are you here in the dark?" It was a rhetorical question, but Evelynn's face spoke of the deepest despair.

"Honey, I need you to come with me."

"No. I don't want to... I can't, Gwen."

Gwen came and knelt in front of her best friend and clasped her hands. "You look beautiful," she smiled gently. She reached up and wiped away the tears from her cheeks.

"Come on... You are going to have to put this gorgeous dress away and save it for another time."

Evelynn turned her face away, new tears spilling over. "There won't be another day."

"Evie, I need you to come back to the hospital with me."

"No, Gwen. Please don't make me. I'm not ready. I can't say goodbye."

"Listen to me... he moved his fingers. You need to get back to the hospital right away."

"But the doctor's said..."

"Well, obviously, your fiancé isn't listening to what the doctors are saying." Tears spilled down Gwen's cheeks as she coaxed her friend from the chair. "Come on. He needs you. He needs to hear your voice."

"Are you sure?"

Gwen pulled her to her feet. "I'm sure! I'm sure! Let's get you out of this thing already!"

"He's going to make it?"

"I don't know! Let's get there and find out! He's fighting, Evie. He's fighting for you. Can we *please* get going?"

Evelynn stood shaking, fresh tears forming. "He's gonna make it? He's gonna make it.... He's gonna make it! I.... I need to be there! Help me out of this dress, will you please?"

Gwen smiled, "Now you're talking!"

Gwen and Evelynn arrived at the hospital breathless. Evie had thrown on some jeans and a bulky sweater. Her hair was still pulled up and fresh snowflakes rested on top trying not to melt. Her face had rivers of make-up, even after she had tried to wipe it clean on the drive over. They were stopped by the doctor at the door. He was leaving Dave's room just as the girls were trying to get in.

"You made it," he smiled.

"Is... is he awake? He's going to make it?' Evelynn asked.

"He is." He held up his hand letting them know there was more. "He is heavily medicated and we will be pulling back on those and that will help him function. His vitals look good though. He's a fighter... "

Gwen's and Evelynn's faces were covered in tears, but the doctor's facial expressions never waivered, not even registering their emotional state.

"Please, can we see him?"

The doctor nodded. "Don't be upset if he doesn't recognize you. Sometimes patients take a while to register names, faces and events. Be patient. He may or may not be able to talk right away. He seems to be doing okay answering basic questions with an 'emotions board'. When he does decide to speak, he may ask a lot of questions repeatedly: it is not anything to worry about right now. Do you understand?

Both girls bobbed their heads obediently.

The doctor smiled. "Congratulations. I think we are almost to the finish line."

"Thank you," Gwen shook his hand as Evelynn was already opening the sliding glass door to his room.

Evelynn stopped at the doorway and smiled. Her fiancé was sitting up in bed with his eyes open. Her heart swelled with joy and it took every ounce of restraint not to run across the room, jump on his bed and throw her arms around his neck. David... her David... he was going to make it.

She couldn't stop crying and opened her mouth to speak when he turned to look at her, but her words were halted when Helen spoke:

"Girl, don't even bother. He's so drugged up right now. I don't even know what they are doing to him, I swear."

She crossed the room and stood by his bed. She put her dainty hand on his. His eyes followed her movements. "David..." she said his name softly.

He brought his eyes up to hers. As she smiled and stroked his cheek, he searched his brain for recognition.

"It's okay," she continued undaunted. "You've been through a lot."

Helen chuffed and Walter attempted to silence her.

"I'm here. You're going to be okay."

Evelynn startled and looked down as David's fingers weakly wrapped around her own.

Tears slipped from her eyes, down her cheeks and onto their entwined hands. She nodded. "Yes, my love. I'm here."

Chapter Fourteen

Every day, Dave got a little stronger, but he didn't attempt to speak. And every day, Helen was there to make sure he didn't have many opportunities to.

The doctors were slowly reducing his pain medications and his organs were getting more independent.

Begrudgingly, he participated in physical therapy at least three times a day. He never complained, but his silent tears spoke of the pain he endured.

While his appetite increased on hospital food, Nick was guilty of sneaking in French fries or slipping him bites from his Blizzard from the local Dairy Queen as rewards.

"What?" he defended, "He's had a rough time of it. Man cannot survive on Pedialite alone."

Whenever Evelynn was in the room, Dave's eyes would follow her, and when she was close enough, he would turn his hand over and open his fingers so she would hold his hand.

"How do you like that?" Helen would complain. "I gave birth to him and he pays me no mind. Barely even knows I'm in the room."

"And a man shall leave his father and mother and be joined to his wife..." Walter paraphrased Ephesians. He was happy in all things and even his own wife couldn't stop him from smiling.

Evelyn paid her little attention as well, and was happy to pour affection on him whenever he requested it.

Evelynn began staying over night at the hospital since Dave was prone to horrific nightmares as he slept.

She didn't feel that an unfamiliar staff would bring him as much comfort as a familiar face, so she opted to stay with him.

Evelynn would be there to stoke his hair and whisper or sing into his ear until he calmed down. If that didn't work, or if it was particularly intense, the nurses would be close by to help with sedation.

"Don't you give up on me David Ripke. You keep fighting, you hear me?" she would coo to him. "I have this amazing wedding dress that I am waiting to wear. You got out of the first wedding... pretty clever. A little extravagant perhaps," she smiled as she ran her finger along the edge of his ear, "and sure, it worked for a minute, but I will have my wedding day, sir," she teased. She kissed his forehead.

"Don't frown at me," she kissed him again and smoothed his worry lines with her thumb. "Lucas is over his *Wizard of Oz* theme. Now, he wants us to get married on Christmas.," she rolled her eyes. "ON Christmas."

"He sees me... riding in on a donkey and getting married in a manger." She shook her head. "While not as extravagant as a glittery horse... or was it a unicorn? I can't keep up... I'm still not comfortable with the whole baby Jesus motif for a wedding."

She held his hand with one of her own and traced along each of his fingers with her own as she chatted away. "You should hear your mom and Lucas in the same room. "It's ridiculous."

She rolled her thumb over his. "Maybe we should just elope. Our 'simple wedding' seems to have slipped away from us." An evil smile crossed her face as her thought came to mind. "Oh, your mom would be so mad!" she laughed thinking about Dave and her driving off down the highway toward the sunset leaving Helen and Lucas fuming in the parking lot. "Maybe, if we're lucky, it will snow on them," she giggled, mixing her inner thoughts with her outer voice.

She sighed and leaned her head against his arm. "I just want to be with you... and start our life. And sleep in our own bed... our own house..." She smiled at him. His eyes were focused on her. She leaned in to kiss him... She suddenly gasped and pulled away from him quickly pinching her brows together.

"You kissed me back!" she gasped. Her eyes filled with tears. "You kissed me back." She leaned in for another, just to make sure she wasn't imagining things. "Oh! Oh, my love..." She kissed him and kissed him again... until the monitors started beeping loudly.

She pulled away and quickly raised her arms in the air innocently.

"I'm sorry! I'm sorry! What'd I do?"

The monitors quieted down to a normal, steady beeping and when she looked back down at her fiancé, he was smiling.

It was getting late. Evelynn fought to keep her eyes open. She and Dave were laying on their sides, facing each other, holding one hand through the safety rail while the DVD of The Bakersfield Fine Arts Centre's production of *Annie Get Your Gun* played quietly in the background on the high corner television.

Dave watched as Evelynn's eyes grew heavier and heavier. He squeezed her hand and her eyes opened in response.

Dave opened his mouth to speak and attempted to force words or sound to come out.

Evelynn propped herself up on her other arm. "Are you alright? Do you need something?"

He smiled and nodded trying to vocalize his thoughts again. A raspy, growling sound escaped, but Evelynn was unable to recognize any words. "Do you want me to get your chart? You can point to…" She tried to pull away but he held her still by squeezing her hand and shaking his head 'no'.

She leaned in, "Okay, try again. I'm listening."

He successfully made a series of grunts and growls linked together to form an incoherent sentence.

"Slow down.,. slow down. Try again. I'm sorry, let me listen again."

She leaned in closer.

He cleared his throat, "How..." he growled low.

"How?" she squealed, "Did you say 'how'?"

"How... did... we do?" He pushed the words out and was breathless. He coughed and had to clear his throat, but he was smiling.

Evelynn was so excited. "How did we do?" she laughed. "You asked 'How did we do?' I heard that! That was so great!" She smiled through her tears. "What... what do you mean... the show? The play?" She glanced back over her shoulder indicating the DVD playing.

He shook his head and tugged on her hand to draw her closer still. "Did..." he swallowed. "Did... we..." He had to pause to catch his breath and clear his throat.

"Did we..." she repeated.

He nodded. "...get..."

She furrowed her brow trying to decipher the sentence. "Did we get..."

He pulled her close to him again. "Did we... get... Hot Stuff?"

Evelynn's jaw dropped and she pushed away from him, her mouth gaping open. Her face turned red and she stared at him speechless.

He laughed. "You... you... you're blushing,.."

"Oh! Oh David!" She threw herself over the bed railing to put her arms around his neck. Her body got 'cut in half' by the railing but she didn't care. He grimaced in pain but weakly he held her body in place when she tried to lift herself off him.

"That's... a.... yes," he rasped breathlessly.

She laughed as she buried her face into his neck His body was so frail and he had lost so much weight and she knew she was probably crushing him, but he wouldn't let her go. "Marry me..." he whispered. "Will... you... marry me?" He pushed the words out and coughed.

"Of course I will!" she laughed! "You can hardly escape it now!" she kissed his cheek. "Do you want to at least wait until you're out of this bed?"

He shook his head 'no'. "Waited... long ... enough."

She pushed herself off him and braced her body with her arms on either side of his head. "Should I go fetch the chaplin, then?" She smiled down on him.

He nodded... "Yes." But then a second later shook his head, "No," He looked over every part of her face as if seeing it for the first time. "Your dress..."

"It's just a dress..."

"You... are... so beau... beautiful. No one... will ... believe you... married... me... without... a wedding." He smiled broadly. "Proof."

She laughed, "You're so silly. I'm the lucky one." She leaned down and kissed him, so happy that he could return such a simple, taken-for-granted- token of affection. It seemed like years.

A wedding. Finally. They would have their simple wedding in Bakersfield.

"A walker? Oh no, honey, we can't have that." Lucas threw his hands in the air, disgusted. "Walker's are for old people. And they'll mess up my photographs... A walker? Really? Baby, can't you just try a little harder?"

"Lucas," Evelynn proceeded calmly, "Walkers can also be for people who have recently come out of medically induced comas and who are impatient to get married and don't want to wait for the additional six months of physical therapy before that can happen."

Lucas was just about to whine again, when his face lit up. "A sleigh!" His eyes went glassy as he got lost deeper into his thoughts. "We can still use that beautiful white horse... add faux snow... and... "

"Lucas..." Dave slurred.

"Simple." Evelynn added.

"Oh honey, it'll be so simple. We just build a ramp down the center aisle..."

"Half.... budget.... Gone." Dave spoke sternly.

Lucas gasped as if he found out his leather jacket was a fake. "You wouldn't."

Dave raised his eyebrow and with great effort said, "I would."

"Faux snow falling from the rafters?"

"As beautiful as that might be, there's enough snow on the *outside* that I'm sure our guests won't need to see it on the inside as well. "

"You want an outdoor wedding?" Lucas asked confused, "... cause the sleigh thing..."

The couple exasperatedly shook their heads "no".

"Lucas crossed one leg over the other and pouted. "I am just too fabulous for this small town."

"I believe that you are." Evelynn smiled. "You are so full of excitement and ideas... but unfortunately, we've been though enough excitement for a while." She reached out a hand and placed it on his knee. "You understand, don't you?"

He raised his hands in defeat, "Alright, alright, love. Simple is what you want. Simple is what you get. So... let's talk flowers..."

Nick walked into Dave's hospital cell carrying a tray of chilled assorted juice cups. He set them down on the rolling table situated across Dave's hospital bed.

Nick chose an orange juice cup for himself and handed the same to Gwen.

"A toast!" he announced, as he pulled back the foil top.

Helen and Walter each grabbed a cup and as Dave was reaching for an orange juice, Evelynn slapped his hand away. "Nope, apple juice for you. It's less acidic."

"See how she treats me?" Dave complained and smiled at the same time, happy for the "abuse".

Evelynn pulled back the foil for her fiancé. "Woman, I can…"

"Just let me," Evelynn stated, "because once you're out of here, you're on your own. So you might as well let me pamper you for a few more days," she teased.

"A toast," Nick repeated now that everyone was ready. The group raised their plastic juice cups in the air. "Here's to… never giving up. To… fighting for what makes life worth living. To friendship and finally," he pulled his own fiancée close to him, "Here's to true love and may it last forever." He nodded to Walter and Helen, and then to Dave and Evelynn.

Dave took Evelynn's hand into his and kissed the back of it.

"Here here!" the group called out and clinked their cups together in the center and drank them.

Helen grimaced, "Ugh! That's the worst cranberry juice I've ever tasted."

Gwen collected everyone's cup and tossed them in the small grey trashcan.

"We've been through a lot together, brother," Nick shook Dave's hand, "I look forward to a lot more."

"Maybe not quite this thrilling, maybe?" Gwen nudged her boyfriend.

"Agreed," he conceded and leaned over to kiss her head.

"Is there any orange juice left?" Helen complained. "I have to get this taste out of my mouth."

"Speaking of..." Dave continued, paying no mind to his mother, "I had the weirdest dream. Remember that..." he looked over at Evelynn, catching himself before uttering an expletive, "... that uh... uh... kid from camp? Billy Croup? He came up in my dreams." Dave shook his head struggling to recall more.

Nick did his best not to make any specific expressions. "Huh... weird..."

"I like totally forgot about him..." He paused before speaking more on the subject, "I would have totally fought him. Would have gotten my ass kicked, but... " he flinched from the gentle scolding smack delivered by Evelynn.

Nick smiled and nodded, "I know you would have, and I would have been right there to make sure your beating didn't get too out of hand."

Dave laughed, "My best friend, everybody."

"Do you remember anything else from being asleep?" Walter asked his son.

"Some things," Dave shrugged. "Again, not sure if they were real or dreams…"

"Like?" Gwen encouraged him to continue.

"Like… if you guys ever decide to do the play *Our Town*… I'm leaving town. There's no way I'm sitting through that again!   And thank goodness I was unconscious for most of it!"

Gwen and Evelynn burst out laughing. "You read *Our Town* to him?" Gwen asked.

Evelynn was laughing so hard that she could barely speak, "People kept saying that it was a classic!" She wiped a tear from her eye. "I forgot how boring it was. It almost made me unconscious too! I'm so sorry, honey," she laughed and kissed his forehead.

"Do you remember me being here?" Helen asked.

Dave nodded.   "Apparently you haven't liked a gift I've given you in the past eight years or so?"

"Helen. Why… just… why?" Walter looked to the heavens for answers.

"What? I didn't know he could hear me. But, I mean, seriously though, how could he not know what I like and don't like?"

Walter closed his eyes and shook his head knowing that words would be useless.

"But mostly," Dave continued, ignoring his parents, "I heard my Evie's voice. Most of the time I couldn't understand what she was saying. Like..." he searched his thoughts for the right words, "... like... I was underwater, but I could still hear her."

Evelynn lifted their entangled hands to her lips and kissed his fingers, trying not to cry.

"Then, suddenly," he looked into her eyes, "I couldn't hear you. I felt like I was being pulled away. It was dark and voices were growing faint... I knew I had to come and find you." A tear slipped from the corner of his eye and ran down his cheek.

She reached for his face to wipe away his tear. "My love. I was afraid... I couldn't bear ... I just knew they were going to tell me that I lost you."

"I know. I understand," Dave nodded, lost in the moment with her. "You have had to be so strong for so long, and that was too much to ask from you. I'm sorry I put you through that." He pulled her down to him for a deep embrace that relayed the relief of their months of separation finally ending.

"Seriously? You know there are other people in the room, right?"

"Helen. Why can't you just be happy for them?"

"I am happy for them. I just don't need to see all that mushy stuff."

Evelynn's phone chirped from her bag.

"Do you need to get that?" Dave asked, reluctantly letting her go.

She shook her head, "Unknown number."

The phone rang through and then the phone went silent. "See? They didn't even leave a message," she shrugged.

"But what if..."

"If it was an emergency, they would call Gwen or Betty. Are you trying to get rid of me?" she pulled back teasing him.

Evelynn's phone went off again. Same ringtone. A moment of panic ran through her, but she looked around and reminded herself that the most important people in her life were right here in this room. The phone quieted again, but this time left a message.

Evelynn's brain started whirring as she tried to act nonchalant but flipping through possible people scenarios for a mystery message.

"Why don't you go ahead and check it before your head explodes," Dave teased.

"But I'm here with you..." she hesitated before her phone went off again.

She grabbed it from her bag and looked at the number. She glanced over at Gwen confused, "It's local."

"Then answer..." Gwen began, but then her own phone rang. She looked down at the lit up screen. "It's Betty."

Evelynn furrowed her brow, "Not again." She looked over at her fiancé, just to make sure he was still there... and breathing.

Gwen and Evelynn answered their phones at the same time. "Hello?"

Their facial expressions almost perfectly mirrored each others. They both took a step back away from their mates as their eyes widened in horror. They looked at each other as their heart beats raced in unison.

"We'll be right there."

Gwen was the first to speak to the others in the room. "We have to go."

Evelynn shoved her phone into the back pocket of her jeans. She leaned over to kiss her boyfriend and paused, not wanting to utter the words, "I... I have to go."

"The theatre..."

"It's on fire..."

Nick, Gwen and Evelynn all ran from the room and down the hall.

Dave shook his head, "My girl... she just can't catch a break." Then he did the only thing that was in his power to do. He prayed.

Chapter Fifteen

By the time Nick pulled his truck into the theatre's parking lot, the fire could be seen slowly and methodically eating through the back roof of the building. They could feel the heat from the flames inside the truck with the windows up.

The street was lined with cars of spectators who decided to pull over and watch, cell phones pointed at the spectacle.

Evelynn jumped out of the truck and looked up at the blaze in awe.

Streams of water came from fire trucks set up on both sides of the building trying to contain the fire. The pressure from the hoses shot roof tiles in every direction.

Two men with hoses stood on the ground shooting upwards attempting to keep the back wall of the theatre's workshop in tact. Bricks crumbled to the ground as layers upon layers decided to give in to the heat.

A third fire truck from a neighboring county pulled up and made it's way through the crowd of people and cars to add still another stream.

The crowd reacted as a section of the roof fell into the building.

The police pushed the crowds back and issued warnings.

Nick, Gwen and Evelynn stood at the front of his truck in silence, for there were no words.

If they tuned out the cacophony of noises around them, the front of the building looked peaceful. All calm and in order. But if you dare to lift your eyes to the night sky, a person couldn't even begin to estimate the amount of damage done to the small town theatre.

Evelynn held her hands to her mouth just trying to grasp the event as it unfolded in front of her. She had run from the hospital without grabbing her coat, and now, as she slowly attempted to walk ever closer to her beloved building, she could feel the skin melting heat from the front and the blisteringly cold air piercing her from the back.

Sweat poured from every opening and she was feeling dizzy with every step. This could not be happening.

Gwen, feeling a similar reaction, caught up to her friend and partner, grabbing her hand, pulling it close to her chest. Both women were speechless, but no words were necessary. Tears streamed down Gwen's face as they stood helplessly and relied completely on the professionals to do their very best to keep the damage at a minimum.

Luckily, the theatre was self-sustained and stood alone on it's own parking lot. The businesses that were remotely close were safe from any damage.

The firemen and police officers worked tirelessly through the night with the flames finally giving in and turning to ashes. Gwen and Evelynn did as they were told and kept their distance, silent spectators, but their expressions spoke volumes as they held each other to brace against the heat and the cold.

Nick brought them an emergency blanket and wrapped the two, knowing that it would be impossible to move either one. He left them to the comfort of one another and made his way over to the fire chief to speak with him now that things looked, for the most part, like they were contained.

As the night wore on, crowds cleared, hoses were emptied and rolled up, trucks gathered up their teams and ladders were withdrawn.

Nick could be seen in the distance speaking to the fire chief. Evelynn and Gwen retreated to the tailgate of Nick's truck; their faces dry from the heat and lack of tears, watched with blank expressions as curling columns of smoke twisted around each other disappearing into the moonless winter sky.

Each was lost in her own thoughts as to what this disaster meant to them, their future, and what was going to happen next. Even though no words were spoken, so tight was their working friendship that their thoughts were surprisingly similar.

Evelynn's head was pounding. She was straining to hear what the fire chief was telling them. He stood before them waiving his arm at the charred building behind him, but the words just weren't getting through. His voice was fading in and out... "...sixty percent of the theatre area is damaged..."

Her body shook with shivers or muscle spasms, she couldn't tell the difference anymore...

"...classrooms and kitchens were spared...offices have...."

Her stomach flipped over and she swallowed the bile that was forcing its way up.

"... seems to have started..."

"Wait, what? What did you say?" her teeth chattered as she tried to form the sentence.

"We believe the fire started because of ..."

"Candles?   Did I..." Evelynn interrupted, fearing the worst.

"No, ma'am. We did find candles, but they were already burned down inside their containers."

"...fabric, left on a light bulb over a period of time... ignited... chemicals in the workshop... paint and such..."

She heard Gwen ask a question.

"Yes, ma'am... the rooms alongside the stage have had some damage."

The dressing rooms... Evelynn calculated.

Gwen was talking... "... items inside..."

"I'm sorry ma'am... nothing in those side rooms could be salvaged. If the fire didn't get it, the water hoses did."

She felt Gwen stiffen next to her, "Oh no...." something... something... "... her wedding dress..."

Evelynn threw back the blanket from her shoulders and slid off the truck's tailgate. She barely made it to the culvert along the edge of their parking lot before she lost control of her stomach contents. Her body involuntarily dropped her to her knees doubling her over in muscle spasms. When her body finally stopped convulsing, Gwen helped her to her feet and wrapped her completely in the blanket.

"Here... here's some tissues," Gwen offered. "Are you alright? Your skin is burning up. We need to get you home and into bed."

Evelynn shook her head. "No... I can't... I need to..." she took two more steps before she slipped from Gwen's grasp and fell to the ground.

When Evelynn woke up, her nose was pressed to the wall and her body felt like it was swaddled in blankets. A moment of panic shot through her and her heart skipped a beat as she struggled to free her arms from under the heavy blanket. She pulled her head back away from the wall to get some kind of perspective.

A lilac colored wall with white butterflies seemed to be her captors wall decoration of choice. She took in a deep breath and sighed.

She lifted her head, attempting to look behind her and saw that her assumptions were correct.

"Max! Get off me!"

At the sound of his name, the wolf-like dog lifted his head which was comfortably positioned near Evelynn's feet, as he was using them for a pillow. Which of course meant... his backend...

She wriggled and squirmed enough to shift her shoulder and release one arm. There, at eye level, a huge bushy tail thumped in happiness at her attention.

"C'mon, Max, get off! I can't breathe!" She flailed her one arm to no avail.

"Auntie Evie! You're awake! Max was protecting you," nine year old Erin squealed.

"He did a great job, but could you get him off so I can move?"

She laughed, "He likes to do that. I'll get Momma..." and she skipped away from the doorframe.

"Wait... could you..." Evelynn dropped her head back down on the pillow with one useless arm above the covers.

Not to allow an unused hand go to waste, Max rose to his feet and made a tight turn, using Evelynn's body parts for leverage wherever necessary to get his nose underneath the limp hand.

"Max!! You are NOT light!" But even as she yelled, her fingers automatically and obediently scratched the beast's head.

Moments later, Gwen came around the corner wiping her hands on a dishtowel. "Hey... hi..." Gwen smiled.

"Hi yourself, kidnapper..."

Erin slipped her head under Gwen's arm, "Did you kidnap Auntie Evie, Momma?"

Gwen shrugged, "Kinda."

"If you could be so kind…" Evelynn pointed to the bladder crushing blockade draped across her body.

"Erin, could you please take Max outside so Aunt Evie can breath again?"

Erin burst out laughing as if that was the funniest thing she'd heard in weeks. "Yeah, he likes to lay on people. C'mon Max…" she cooed. He thumped his tail but was in no mood to vacate the bed or the affection. "Maxey… you wanna go outside? Do ya? You wanna go play? C'mon, boy…"

"Max," Gwen spoke sternly. "Get down."

The dog literally huffed. He yawned before getting to his feet and bent his front paws low as he stretched out the back half. Evelynn cried out from the abuse. He slowly, in absolutely no rush what-so-ever, extended two paws to the floor… one more stretch before the back paws followed suit. He stood beside the bed and looked up at Gwen as if to say, "Are you happy now?"

Undeterred, Erin weakly snapped her fingers and called, "Good boy, Maxey! Let's go!"

The wolf followed the tiny human out of the bedroom.

"Oh, my bladder!" Evelynn complained.

Erin stuck her head back in the room. "Can Aunt Evie come and play too?"

"Not now," Gwen said over her shoulder as she sat at the end of the twin bed, draped in Merida sheets.

"But she's been asleep forever!"

Gwen looked at her best friend and mouthed, "Forever!"

"Are we kidnapping her again tomorrow?"

"No," Evelynn interjected.

Gwen smiled at her friend, accepting the challenge. "We'll see."

"'Cause we can watch *Tangled* and *Cinderella*... and... and *Moana*... that's your favorite..."

Evelynn smiled back at the sweet little face, "It sure is."

"Go play..." Gwen shot the order and the child disappeared from the door but could be heard singing down the hall... "I am Moana!!!"

"So," Gwen turned her attention back to the inmate, "How ya feeling?"

"Like I've been run over by a truck."

"Not surprised, you've been out for two days."

"Two days! Dave! What about... two days? The theatre! Was it... was it a dream? Why am I at your house?"

Gwen raised her hand to calm her friend. "Whoa, whoa... all the answers you seek will be given to you in time, grasshopper," Gwen smiled. "But first go to the bathroom, and for all of our sakes, brush your teeth, then meet me in the kitchen and I shall feed you."

Evelynn couldn't help but laugh. "Don't suppose I could get a whole shower?"

"Please!" Gwen overreacted. "There's a change of clothes and you know your way around for everything else. Dave is expecting your call whenever, so go ahead and take your time." She patted the leg under the blanket lovingly. "I'll go make breakfast."

"I don't know if I can..."

"You can." Gwen stood and left the room. "Meet you in the kitchen," she called back.

Evelynn was towel drying her hair when she walked to the kitchen and looked out the sliding glass door at Erin and Max playing in the back yard.

"What a pair."

"They are, aren't they." Gwen stopped and followed Evelynn's view. "French toast?" She held up a plate.

"Oh my gosh, those look and smell so good. And real maple syrup? Oh, you do love me... or wait..." she paused sitting at the table, "the news... it's really bad? Dave wouldn't tell me anything."

Gwen shrugged. "How bout a little of both?" Gwen sat in the seat beside her and rested her chin in her hand.

Suddenly, Max started scratching wildly at the back door demanding to be let in.

Evelynn jumped, startled at the fuss.

Gwen smiled. "Nick must be here." She stood and crossed the short distance to the door and slid back the glass before Max went through it. And, as if on cue, the front door opened and the two met in the middle. Max pounced and Nick caught him like the overgrown furry toddler he was.

"Hey, Buddy," Nick nuzzled the wolf. "How's my boy, huh? Miss your Daddy, do ya? Yeah, you do."

He set Max down on his hind legs and Max proceeded to bounce around the room as if it were Christmas morning and he'd just met Santa Claus.

"Gwen!" Nick called into the kitchen, "Guess what the Phoenix Project got approved for next! You'll never guess, so I'll tell you. *Noah's Ark HQ*"

Gwen walked toward him to close the gap. She took advantage of his pause in words to steal a quick kiss.

"Have you ever heard of that?" Kiss.

"Me either." Kiss. "This guy saves all these abandoned animals." He chattered on, not skipping a beat. "I know a lot of people rescue animals, but... he... he... does all the animals. He started saving them at his house and soon got so many that his neighbors started to complain. The city was going to make him euthanize all of them or find homes for them by a certain date, or find some place to put them, outside of city limits. So..." He grabbed both of Gwen's hands in his own and just noticed Evelynn sitting at the kitchen table eating, "Oh, hey Evie."

She nodded, returning the greeting.

"So, anyway, he took his dilemma to social media. He got so much response that it reached this guy who owned a chain of department stores... uh... uh... *Goldies,* I think. This department store owner donated one of his empty buildings to this guy to house all of his animals. Now, he has this whole building. He's divided it up to have an infirmary, a place for dogs, cats, other miscellaneous creatures... He's... he's changed the covered parking garage into stables for the horses, goats and even cattle. Such a huge undertaking. This guy's heart is so big."

"A Noah's Ark of pets?" Gwen added, getting caught up in his excitement. "What is the *Phoenix Project* going to do?"

"Well, it is a huge project that will always be in need, so we can't do everything. But we decided that we would first raise awareness, of course, so people can donate supplies and food and care for the animals, but I'm pretty sure we've settled on... wait... let me back up..."

"Hold..." Gwen raised her hand, "on that thought... do you want some French toast?" she asked.

Nick huffed, "No..." Gwen looked up at him as if he'd been taken over by aliens... "Of course, I do."

She took his hand and led him over to the kitchen table. "Okay, continue..."

And without skipping a beat, he jumped back into his story. "So, right now the dogs are on the second floor. Plenty of space but..."

Both the women reacted to potential disasters at the implication.

"Exactly. They need a way to get to the ground floor to do their business. I think we are designing... and building a ramp of sorts to accommodate that. We should be able to get that done in about a week. And we will be digging up a portion of the parking lot to create more green space. The whole back half of the parking lot. I mean, really, how many people are going to shop for pets at the same time?" He shrugged his shoulders at the ridiculousness of so many parking spaces. "We've already made some phone calls and have got an architect and engineer on board, plus Ste. Genevieve Hardware and Lumber called us when they found out what we were up to."

Gwen walked up beside him and set a plate in front of him. Nick reached out and put his arm around her waist pulling her into his lap.

"This is going to be *so* great!" He kissed her head. "Thank you for the French toast. I love you."

Gwen giggled. "I love you, too. I am so excited for you. You are doing great things."

"I'm pretty stoked." He kissed her again and helped her back to her feet. As he prepped his breakfast with syrup, he spoke to Evelynn, "Glad to see you up and about. Your boyfriend misses you."

Evelynn blushed, "I know. I'm going to go up there as soon as my captor releases me."

"I'm sorry, Evie," Gwen defended, "You would not have been allowed anywhere near that floor with that fever you had."

Evelynn leaned back in her chair, covering her belly with her hands, already regretting eating those extra pieces of toast. "Whoo..." she pushed her plate further away from her. "That was so good. I can't remember the last time you made me French toast."

"We're always so busy," Gwen shrugged.

"Well, you have plenty of time now," Nick suggested as he shoved in a bite and jotted down notes on his cell phone's notebook.

"What?" Evelynn asked. "Why's that?"

"Well," Nick went on, only half in the conversation, "Rip's getting out of the hospital soon and his parents will be leaving since..." he paused, looking up from his phone and suddenly 'seeing' her. "You sure are taking this well."

"What?" Evelynn grew more uncomfortable with every single second that ticked by.

"The theatre..."

Gwen interrupted, "Uh... honey... we haven't discussed that as yet. Evelynn just woke up and you were all.... *Phoenix Project...* " she waved her hands around trying to wrap up the excitement of the morning. "She literally just woke up."

He looked to Evelynn for confirmation.

"Just," she nodded.

He stared blankly and apologetically at Gwen. He searched for words as he could feel Evelynn's anxiety climb. "Uh... I think this is where I offer to take Erin out for ice-cream."

Gwen couldn't help but giggle at his predicament. "What about your breakfast?"

He grabbed his fork and jammed the equivalent of six bites into his mouth. "Besides," he said around a mouthful of bread, "ith tech-nic-we wuth."

"It's not technically lunch," Gwen scoffed.

Nick gave her the "whatever" look, "Ith two uh cwock."

"Two o'clock!" Evelynn looked at her friends, feeling betrayed. She leaned back on the legs of the chair to see the microwave clock.. "Oh my gosh! I've practically slept away another whole day! Dave didn't even say a thing!" She stood up and took her plate to the sink.

"He knows where you are and that we've been taking care of you," Gwen looked over her shoulder "And that you've been getting the rest that you *need*."

Evelynn was rinsing the stickiness off her plate. "Why are his parents leaving? Aren't they staying for the...." Evelynn shuddered suddenly realizing... remembering. The events of the night of the fire spinning around in her head, she almost lost her balance. The plate crashed in the sink. Her eyes welled up with tears.

Nick, not paying any attention, continued "Since your wedding plans have gone up in smoke, literally, I guess..." Nick looked up and saw the death glare he was getting from his fiancée, but it was the look on Evelynn's face that was his undoing. "I... I'm sorry... I wasn't... I shouldn't... have... uh... I've... uh... we've had time to process... I...   "

"Stop talking, honey."

"I... I will... I'm just... where *is* that child?" He stood up and the dog followed his actions and they both went to the back door. He grimaced at Gwen who could only shake her head.

As Nick ducked out the back door, Gwen went into repair mode. She went to the sink and wrapped her arms around her best friend.

"It wasn't a dream..." Evelynn cried into her shoulder.

Gwen just sighed and held her tighter.

"It's bad?"

Gwen pulled her back and held her by the shoulders. She looked down before she could bear to bring her eyes back up to Evelynn's. "It's bad." She tipped her head to the side. "Come sit down."

They turned toward the living room.

Evelynn was always the strong one. The sensible one. The one who usually takes care of the hard stuff. Gwen was on unfamiliar ground watching *her* rock crumble in front of her.

Evelynn took a deep breath and made her way to the end of the couch. She reached for the tissues on the end table. She grabbed a couple and flopped down on the end of the couch turning inward. She wiped away her tears and blew her nose. She took another deep breath, another couple tissues and faced Gwen. "Okay, I'm ready."

Gwen started by saying that volunteers and students have already been cleaning and removing debris.

"The good news is," she offered, "the offices and the Centre lobby are virtually untouched. The student lounge has a little bit of water damage to the floors, but that's it. And thankfully, the dance floors are unharmed."

Evelynn nodded, thankful for that information, but stayed quiet, knowing that there was more. Whenever her best friend started with the 'good news' she knew that bad was going to be pretty steep.

"All of the flooring and about two feet of the walls has had to come out because of water damage, not from fire. I... uh... I don't know whether that's good or bad, but... uh, like I said, there's been a clean up crew working through out the daylight hours for the last couple days, and the debris is being hauled off almost as fast as we can get it out there. We have certainly been blessed with help."

Silent tears spilled from Evelynn's eyes as she listened, nodding.

"So," Gwen continued, "We just need to let it air out before we can start putting it back together."

Evelynn tried to visualize the situation as Gwen described it and was already thinking of how to get things up and running again.

"And... the theatre?" she dared to ask.

"Well, the good news is..."

Evelynn clenched her teeth waiting for the other shoe to eventually drop.

"...the sound board, curtain and fly systems are all intact. The um... the kitchen is intact also..."

Gwen paused not wanting to continue.

Evelynn took in a deep breath and reached over to her friend who sat facing her and grabbed her hand. "Go ahead, just say it. We can deal with it."

Gwen nodded. "The uh..." Gwen took in a deep breath and pressed it out feeling the tears sting her eyes. "The front part of the stage... gone. About ... two-thirds." She swallowed. "The first three rows of seats, they are... ruined. Rows four through eight probably have some water damage, but I believe are salvageable. Most of the workshop, and the wall between the stage and workshop is down to the metal framing." She involuntarily shrugged as she spoke, not knowing how to fix the pain the words were causing her friend. "It's just a shell..." A tear slipped away.

Evelynn squeezed her hands, "I'm so sorry you had to take all this on yourself. I'm sorry that..."

"Don't. Please don't do that. We're in this together. We always have been."

"But I should have..."

"It's not over. We're not down forever. The guys are in there right now rebuilding the side wall."

"Is there electricity?"

"Some. We're running it from all over the place," Gwen giggled at some of the ingenuity that was in place at the moment.

Evelynn nodded. "Fans?"

"Blowing, and heaters for the workers."

A thought crossed Evelynn's mind and Gwen cringed already knowing what was coming and dreading the answer.

"The dressing rooms?"

Gwen took in a deep breath and shook her head. "Mostly gone, by either fire or water."

Evelynn nodded blankly. "My... dress is..."

"Honey, we can make another one... just as beautiful."

Evelynn dropped her head, willing herself not to shed one more tear. "His parents are leaving..." as if it was all coming together.

"Evie," Gwen pleaded, "It could have been so much worse."

She nodded.

"No one was hurt. That is a blessing in and of itself."

She nodded.

"And... and... we are working on rebuilding..."

Evelynn shot her a serious glance. "Oh yes. We've built it once, we can build it again."

Gwen smiled. "There's my girl. Plus, we have a bigger support system, government funding... and I happen to have this amazing, handsome future husband that *LOVES* projects like this..."

All of a sudden Evelynn reached her limit and broke down. Gut wrenching wails and crocodile tears came from the slim dancer's body.

"Evie... honey..." Gwen scooted closer and lifted her friend's head. She took the tissue from her hands and wiped her cheeks... "Hey... it's going to be okay..."

"You... you were... waiting..." Evelynn bawled, "for me to ... get married first." She gasped for air, "And now... it's been put off a-geh-heh-hen...."Her chest heaved with sobs and she just couldn't stop. "Maybe I'm not supposed to be married," she screeched.

"Stop. You stop that train of thought right now. I've never seen a happier couple..."

"Except for you and Nick..."

"Well, yes, of course we're happy but..."

"Maybe you can... still save your wedding. You can... can..." she hiccupped, "elope."

Gwen pulled away and rolled her eyes. "Really? We've come through all this and you think we're just going to run off and elope?" Gwen paused for a moment to let the scenario run it's course. "Unless... You and Dave want to elope too..." she wiped away the new tears, "We *could* get married at the same time..."

"The way my luck is going, the plane would crash before we got there!" she sobbed.

Gwen shrugged trying not to give into tears herself, "Who wants to get married by Elvis anyway."

Evelynn sniffed, "I'm so sorry. I feel like I've ruined everything,"

Gwen wrapped her arms around her friend. "Okay, now you're just being silly. None of this has been in your control. Things just happen. You haven't ruined anything." They rocked silently for a moment, not even realizing the soothing swaying motion had begun. "Why on earth would you start doubting your faith now? This isn't the first time we've been laid low. Now is not the time to abandon faith. He tells us that this is when we need it most. Now is the time we lean into Him and let Him take the lead."

Evelynn pushed back, creating a space between the two of them. "Who are you and what have you done with my Gwen?" she sniffled.

Gwen smiled, "I've been reluctantly listening to my best friend every once in a while, but shhh, don't tell her." Gwen glanced sideways at Evelynn. "In fact," Gwen set the stage for the final strike, "She has this plaque hanging in her office."

Evelynn rolled her eyes, knowing what was coming and smiled as she accepted the gentle scolding.

"It says" Gwen looked away searching her memory, "Isaiah 41:10. *So do not fear, for I am with you; do not be dismayed for I am your God. I will strengthen you and help you...*"

Evelynn joined in and finished the verse with her, "*I will uphold you with my righteous right hand.*"

They leaned forward and touched foreheads.

"This best friend of yours," Evelynn spoke softly, "she must be pretty amazing."

Gwen giggled, "On most days."

Gwen decided to drive her truck in the back entrance of the theatre since that's where the bulk of the damage occurred.

Evelynn involuntarily brought her hand to cover her mouth as something similar to a burning, tingling sensation pricked her skin. She could feel her stomach revolt, but fought to keep her food down. She prayed for peace and strength and felt a calm come over her, and then she knew she would have those things when she truly needed them. He was with her, just as He promised.

Huge, black, charred rafters jutted from the top of the steeped building. Twisted metal burst into the sky and the sun bounced off it's melted edges and sent sparks of rainbow light in all directions. It almost looked like a new world artistic piece.

The closer they got, Evelynn could see the gaping hole that was eaten away by flames. The cutaway dipped a bit down the back wall exposing a section of the workshop as well. It looked like the theatre version of a doll-house; the hole just large enough so a giant hand could reach in and rearrange furniture.

Both doors of the workshop were wide open and Evelynn could see movement inside.

She didn't realize that Gwen had stopped the truck to allow her to take it all in. She watched for a moment as some children, a few she recognized from her dance classes, others from Gwen's drama class, were singing and pushing water towards the parking lot with firm bristled push brooms. One of them spotted the truck and waved wildly. Gwen smiled and waved back while Evelynn was struggling to breathe.

"Are you ready to go in?" Gwen asked gently, shifting the gears to drive. Evelynn shook her head vehemently. She suddenly wanted to go back home and put her head under the covers and pray that it was just a bad dream.

"C'mon," Gwen grabbed Evelynn's hand. "Everyone needs to see you. They've all been praying for you."

Evelynn turned to her and looked like a frightened puppy.

"They need to see that you are okay."

"I was so brave just a few moments ago," Evelynn lamented. "And suddenly, now, I don't feel... okay." Her voice cracked.

"Well, you have about thirty seconds to *get* okay... or at least be ready to fake it... You don't have to be one hundred percent. No one expects that." Gwen pulled into a spot next to several other vehicles. Gwen reached onto the dashboard to grab two sets of work gloves and elbowed her best friend. "Time's up."

Gwen tossed a pair of gloves to her co-pilot, which, Evelynn completely missed and they ended up smacking her in the face.

Gwen couldn't help but giggle, "Ready?"

Evelynn looked at her, "The show must go on?" She quoted from the recently closed *Annie Get Your Gun*.

Gwen nodded. "The show must go on."

Evelynn took a deep breath and nodded, resolved and ready to face whatever waited for her on the other side of those doors.

No sooner had she crossed the threshold of the main entrance, the smell of wet and mildew accosted her, even though the doors were propped open with bricks.

She was quickly spotted and showered with love. Students, parents and co-workers greeted her with hugs and kind, loving words. She was once again overwhelmed and could feel the warm tears relieve the stinging in her eyes and the coolness of her cheeks.

The lobby was untouched and long tables were set up along one wall. On one were cases of water bottles, snacks, plates, plasticware, along with a temporary steam table that housed spaghetti, green beans and buttered noodles. On another table, spare gloves and tools were at the ready. A large poster board was at the very end of the length of tables. It was covered with the signatures of the people who had stopped in to help. Evelynn's heart swelled as she looked around at everyone's faces and all that had all ready been done.

The lobby was saved from any damage and as Evelynn looked around taking in her surroundings, she was so thankful that her collection of paintings she'd collected throughout her life still hung safely on the walls. But that smell...stale water. Water trapped in carpet... and just like that... she was back.

She raised her hand to quiet the room, which had slowly filled to thirty or forty people. "Ladies and gentlemen," she began, swallowing the lump in her throat, "Oh... I am so thankful that you are all here. I don't know if I could have done this by myself... seeing it for the first time. I appreciate all of your kind words and your unwavering support in my absence this past month or so. It would seem like a few things have changed a bit."

There was quiet laughter that crossed the room.

She swallowed, "You know, I've been wanting to upgrade that lighting system for years," she laughed feebly, "Looks like the time has come."

Nick had come up and slid his arm around Gwen's waist while she leaned against a wall in the background.

The crowd responded warmly and once again she felt that calm warm her body.

"Alright then," she slipped on her work gloves. "Let's see what needs to be done. Can you show me the way?"

The group rallied it's support and a handful went before her to 'lead the way'.

Gwen smiled, as she watched. "She's back," she said under her breath and looked up at her boyfriend. "Enjoy the ice cream?"

Nick rolled his eyes and took the unspoken scolding. "Come on, woman. Let's go get dirty." He bobbed his eyebrows and swatted her behind as she walked past him.

Chapter Sixteen

Gwen walked up to Dave's room and stopped just outside the door. She could see Evelynn and Dave sitting on the edge of the bed, holding hands, with their heads bowed in prayer.

When their heads raised and Evelynn lay her head on Dave's shoulder, she entered the room. "Hey guys, what's up?"

"Dave is being released the day after tomorrow," Evelynn smiled.

"Are they sure? There's been a lot of going back and forth on that."

"They promised," Dave laughed. "I think I've worn them down. They like me much better when I can't talk."

"That's great news!" Gwen cheered leaning in to hug the couple. "Why... uh... why aren't you smiling?"

"I'm smiling. Aren't you smiling, babe?" Dave pulled his neck back trying to see her face still pressed against him.

"I am," Evelynn admitted, "It's just... we weren't sure where Dave would go once he'd been released."

"Oh." Gwen knew her best friend's discomfort right away. She sat in the arm chair across from them to listen. "And what did you decide?"

"He's going to move in with me," Evelynn said.

Gwen said nothing, knowing how her friend felt about it already.

"Yeah, we're shacking up. All the kids are doing it," Dave smirked. But Evelynn did not share in his joke.

"And the wedding?" Gwen politely probed further.

Evelynn sighed heavily. She glanced up at her fiancé before answering. "We're holding off until next year. Next November." There. She said it, and the world really didn't implode.

"Why so long?"

"I know you and you'll want a Spring wedding," Evelynn began. When Gwen tried to protest, Evelynn held up her hand to quiet her. "You've waited long enough." She paused, allowing the seriousness in her tone sink in. "Plus Gillian and Tom are getting married in the summer."

"Has it been two years already?"

Evelynn nodded and smiled. "So much has happened since that earth-shattering Christmas in tiny little Bakersfield."

Gwen furrowed her brow and was suddenly lost in her own thoughts.

"Are you going to cry?" Dave asked.

"She's thinking. That's her thinking face," Evelynn teased. Not sure if it's going backwards, remembering or forward in planning mode." Gwen shot her friend a look. "Don't worry about it, Gwen. Dave and I have talked about it. We'll spend this next year getting the theatre back in order..."

"...plus house hunting," Dave added.

"But..."

"Time will go by quickly. Plus we have to plan for your wedding."

Evelynn blinked back a tear. She really was okay with the idea of waiting, but it just stung a little more than she thought it would saying it to her very best friend who could read her like a book.

Gwen shook her head; "I don't believe you for a moment Evie St. Lawrence."

"How bout... it's what has to be, for now." Evelynn had her executive director face on which told Gwen that she was going to fall back on business mode to push through emotional-disappointment mode.

"Okay." Gwen gave in and shrugged. "What do you need me to do?"

Evelynn slowly lifted her shoulders and let them fall. "Let's just keep the troops rallied and do the next most-important thing."

Gwen winked, clicked her tongue and pointed her index finger at Evelynn. "I'm on it, boss."

Chapter Seventeen

"Oh! Somethin' smellin' rancid in here," Lucas said as he walked down the hall holding his slacks up as if they were a long skirt.

Evelynn paused on her duty of scraping up the water-logged floor tiles from the dressing room floor to address Lucas tip-toeing into the room.

"Hey stranger," she used the back of her glove to wipe her cheek and to remove the escaped hairs from her braid that had gotten stuck to her sweaty face.

"Hey, yourself."

"Did you come to help? Want me to get you some gloves?"

Lucas stopped dead in his tracks and curled up his lip, "Did you just meet me?" He looked around the room as if there would be someone else there to confirm the ridiculousness of her question. "Do you see these hands? They don't stay this soft by messin with no dirty tools. No ma'am, thank you very much. No offense."

"None taken," Evelynn laughed to herself.

"So..." he looked over his surroundings, "you've got the dressing room almost all cleaned out. That's good." He still kept his lip curled up in disgust at having to make his appearance under such conditions. The burdens of friendship.

"Yeah," Evelynn leaned against the scraper, "We cut the water damaged parts of the wall out," she pointed to the bottom edge of the room, "These tiles need to come up," pointing to the remainder of her task, "And the room needs to air out. Thankfully the mirrors are in tact, and..."

"Mmmhmm... where's my girl, Miss Gwen?" he interrupted, not really listening anyway.

"She... uh... last I saw her, she was replacing plywood on the stage?"

"Mmmhmm..." He darted his eyes around the room. "I hope you gonna keep the fans running all the time. Stinks in here."

"Yes, Lucas. Thank you."

"Jus sayin'."

"So... uh... Dave called you?"

"He sure did. Spoke with the Little Man this morning. And honey, I am so sorry things is happening this way. But it's all gone be okay."

She nodded, lowering her eyes. "I know. I just need to be patient."

"Giirrl, I ain't never met anybody more patient and more forgiving than you."

She shrugged. "It'll happen when it's supposed to."

He clicked his tongue, "You got that right."

Evelynn cleared her throat, wanting to change the subject. "So... will you be staying? We could use a great make-up artist around here."

"Girl, you sure could, but you know Lucas Lesley Power's talents be too big for this lil bitty town."

Evelynn laughed. "That... is very true."

"But," Lucas waved his index finger in front of her, "I won't miss your big day for nothin', you hear me?"

She nodded and smiled. "I'm happy to hear that. When things get settled, I'll be sure to let you know what date we've chosen. And... and before you go, you'll have to come over for dinner."

"Oh girl, don't you worry. We'll see each other again before I bounce. But right now, I got to get outta here before my allergies start up. I'm not a pretty crier. Trust me, now."

Evelynn couldn't help but love the giant man daintily grabbing small pinches of fabric between his finger and thumb.

"Lucas, there's no water here."

"Do you know how much these pants cost? You just don't go around sloshing about."

"But there's..."

He shushed her, "You get back to your scrubbing, *Cinderella*."

She popped her eyebrows up at his playful dig.

"Yes, evil step sister," she laughed.

Lucas stopped at the doorway and looked back over his shoulder, smiling, "Ooo, you bad! I love it!"

Evelynn had her cell phone tucked between her cheek and shoulder while she returned the tools back to the edge of the stage.

"Yeah, I think I got pretty much done today," she was saying. "I'm beat, but the dressing room is all cleared out and drying out. Gwen worked on the stage most of the day. She's on fire."

"She's anxious for things to get back to normal, I'm sure," Dave offered.

"Probably. She gets pretty driven and focused when she's onto something."

"What time are you coming to rescue me tomorrow?" he asked.

"I'll try to get there early so I can be there for the last doctor visit and get your prescriptions filled before we leave... oh, and make your first physical therapy appointment *and* I believe the nurses said you'll be able to escape around noon? One?"

"Sounds good to me. I'm ready to be out of this place. Even better that it's just in time for Christmas."

"Wha... what?"

"Christmas... you know that big holiday that comes in December..."

"I know of the holiday, but... honestly... I completely forgot about it."

"So, don't hold my breath for a Christmas present?"

"Uh, sir, I gave you a Christmas present and a birthday present and an every other holiday present and you blew it up."

"Ooo... Ouch!"

Evelynn leaned against the wall. "Honey, I'm sorry. I completely forgot... I don't even have a tree or anything."

"Babe, it's all good. I'm just happy to be spending it with you."

"You are so good to me. I love you."

"I love you, too."

Evelynn took in a deep breath and tried to get back on track. "I'm going to leave here early tonight so I can make some space for you at the house."

"Great. I sleep on the right side," Dave teased knowing that his fiancée was blushing on the other end of the phone."

He could hear her giggle, before she added, "I'll see what I can do. I've got to get off here. I love you."

"I love you, too." A silence hung for a moment. "It's alright. He knows our hearts."

"I... no... yeah, I know that. I just wanted to do everything the 'right' way this time. I did everything wrong, and I mean everything the last time."

"Hey, babe, that time is past. I'm not him..."

"I know, but..."

"These are completely different circumstances."

"I know..."

"If you are really still uncomfortable, I can go back to Nick's place. He already said he had no problems..."

"I know, but... he and Gwen are trying to move on with their lives too..."

Another silent gap... "So... we're good?"

Evelynn felt herself smile at the thought of sleeping next to the man she had fallen in love with. "We are good. I'll see you tomorrow."

"You better." She could hear the smile in his voice before he clicked the end button.

She tucked the phone into her back pocket and made her way into the auditorium to tell Gwen that she was leaving.

She was pacing back and forth on the stage talking on the phone.

"Gwen," Evelynn stage whispered. No response.

She took a few more steps closer. "Gwen," she added a bit of voice. Gwen was still deep in her phone conversation.

Evelynn walked up to the edge of the stage and looked up. "Guienevere!"

"Oh! Oh my chickens!!" Gwen jumped and tossed her phone up in the air. It summersaulted and bounced on the stage floor. "Evie! You scared me! How long have you been standing there?" She looked out of breath as she leaned over and picked up her phone. "Hello? Yeah, sorry about that: I dropped the phone. So... we're good?" She held up her finger to tell Evelynn to hold on for just a sec. "Great. Thank you so much, I really, really appreciate it. Great. Yes. See you then. Thank you." She clicked the button on her phone and looked up at Evelynn, giving her all her attention. "Uh, so... hi."

Evelynn laughed. "You okay?"

"Yeah, you know, just trying to get stuff squared away... and uh... stuff."

Evelynn stared at her for just a second and Gwen knew she sounded ... off.

"I was just coming to tell you that I need to head out a little early tonight. Dave is coming home tomorrow." She smiled and chuffed. "My home... our home." She paused letting that thought sink in. "Did you know Christmas was a couple days away?" She blinked and bonked herself on the head. "I don't know how I missed that."

"You didn't miss it. You just haven't been able to participate." Gwen scrunched her face, "You've been kinda busy."

Evelynn searched her memories. "I do recall the holiday lighting on town square..."

"Christmas music in the stores..."

"The manger in front of the court house..."

"The tree in my living room..."

Evelynn shook her head, "No... I missed that... completely."

"It's my first one in years. I'm surprised Erin didn't drag your sleeping body to lie next to it. If she's quiet for too long, I can usually find her lying under the tree looking up at the lights from underneath. It's so sweet."

"Awww! That is so sweet! I need to get a tree for Dave. I love Christmas trees," she said absent- mindedly.

Gwen came to the edge of the stage and sat down swinging her legs over the side. She touched the side of Evelynn's face. "I'm sure he'll be fine. You've done enough. Let's not worry about trees for now. If you have time after he gets there, great.

You'll probably get a really good deal!" she laughed. Evelynn looked up at her not quiet convinced. She smiled, "It's good. This... you and Dave... it's all going to be okay."

Evelynn shrugged. "Yeah... it is. But I need to get home and give him some space to call his own, you know?"

"Absolutely." They snapped back to business. She folded her hands in front of her. "I'm uh, just going to stay a bit longer. There's a few more things I think I can get done tonight."

"Okay. Thank you. I probably won't see you tomorrow, I'll be wrapped up with doctors and papers and getting Dave settled and then maybe Christmas tree shopping.

Gwen did not respond, but just smiled and saluted.

"You need some sleep," Evelynn frowned at her bestie.

"Pfft! Sleep is for the weak!"

Evelynn laughed and hugged her neck. "Okay, see you when I see you."

"I'm coming!" Evelynn called out to the closed front door. She tied the sash around her robe and sleepily opened her door.

"Good morning!" Gwen stuck her face in the screen door. "You awake?"

Evelynn furrowed her brow and adjusted her vision. "Technically...?" She rubbed her eyes and stepped back away from the door. "Want some coffee? It should start brewing in about... two minutes?"

Gwen pushed opened the door and threw her arms around her best friend's neck. "Nope," she said swaying back and forth, "I'm taking you out for breakfast."

"Why are you taking me out for breakfast?"" Evelynn's voice was muffled in the elbow of Gwen's coat.

"Because, I love you. And you said we weren't going to see each other. I just don't think I could bear that today."

Evelynn allowed herself to be rocked and loved on, but was quietly wondering exactly when her best friend had lost her mind.

Gwen released her and spun her back towards the living room and gave her a push. "Go on, go get some clothes on."

Evelynn looked back over her shoulder but kept moving in the direction she was not so gently nudged.

"And wear a button down shirt." Gwen added.

"What?"

"Go on..."

"Can I wear pants?"

"Of course you can, don't be silly," Gwen rolled her eyes as if this was just a regular day of perfectly normal friend- kidnapping.

As they closed the door of Gwen's truck, ready to head out to the local Chicken Depot for breakfast, Evelynn looked over at Gwen and said, "This can't take long. You know I have a busy day ahead of me."

Gwen looked at her passenger as innocently as she could muster. "Yes, of course. Your day is going to be quite busy. I've got your back."

Evelynn nodded, accepting the answer, but just wasn't settled with the sincerity of it...

The waitress came by their table and held up her coffee pot. "Would you like a refill?"

"Yes, please," Gwen scooted her cup closer to the edge.

Evelynn waived her hand over her cup signifying that she had capped off. "Another cup? You're going to float away!"

"We don't get to do this very often," Gwen shrugged. She leaned across the table and grabbed Evelynn's hands, "Let's go get manicures!"

Evelynn frowned at her. "What is wrong with you today? You know I have to pick Dave up from the hospital. He's been locked up there long enough."

"I know, but..."

Evelynn's phone went off. She glanced at the screen, "It's Dave, do you mind?"

Gwen shrugged.

Just then Gwen's phone chimed too.

A brief moment of panic flashed in Evelynn's eyes. She's had one too many experiences where this was the prelude to something very bad.

But Gwen's expression was different. She was not surprised.

They both grabbed their phones and leaned back in their booth.

After a moment, Evelynn looked up at Gwen questioningly, "You wouldn't happen to know why Nick is at the hospital, would you?"

Gwen wouldn't make eye-contact. Evelynn gasped. "Are you pregnant?"

Gwen looked up at her friend, shocked and slightly insulted. "Absolutely not! Do you really think me as weak as that?"

Evelynn cocked an eyebrow, knowing this woman down to her core.

"Okay, fine, but no... I'm not." Gwen rolled her eyes, "Pfft, pregnant... really?"

Evelynn shrugged her shoulders. "You are acting really weird this morning, so it has to be something pretty big if you feel you need to go through all of this..."

"Ummmm..." Gwen looked everywhere but across the table.

"Gwen?" No answer. "Gwen, you are a terrible liar... maybe you should just fess up?"

Gwen bit her bottom lip and leaned forward. She took the phone from Evelynn and cupped her hands in her own. "Today.... "

The pause was too long, "Yes?   Today, what? Out with it."

Gwen's shoulder bounced up and down nervously... "You are getting married today."

Evelynn was lead into the dressing room by way of the office doors. She was ordered to keep her head down and just walk down the hallway to the designated room. She waffled between tears of happiness and tears of confusion, but quietly, well, mostly, did what she was told.

When she got to the dressing room that she had just cleaned out the day before, it was lit up with Christmas lights around the make-up mirrors. A card table had a fruit tray, a meat and cheese tray and three bottles of champagne chilling in a bucket of ice.

Evelynn drew in a breath at the site. "What have you done, Gwen Collins? This is so... I don't deserve..."

"Oh, but you do. Plus, if you don't get married, I don't get to get married, so I thought I'd help things along," she teased.

Evelynn shoved her friend in the shoulder.

"Hey! We thought we heard you come in," Gillian called from the door. Her best friend Rae, who also happened to be everyone's hair stylist stood beside her.

"Hey Gill," Gwen smiled and greeted. "Okay, I did my part, I got her here. Now, work your magic."

Rae stepped up and hugged Evelynn, "I'm going to do your hair, if that's okay. I know we haven't had much of a chance to discuss what you want, but I can pull up some pictures for you."

"And I," Gillian dabbed Evelynn's face with a tissue, "… am going to do your make-up, if you could just please stop crying for a minute." She also hugged her co-worker and friend.

"But… I don't understand… how did… what have…"

"We've got this," Gwen escorted her to a high stool that swiveled away from the mirror. "Now, gimme your hands. Since you refused a mani-pedi, I guess I'm going to have to do it."

"But…"

"Shush."

"But the theatre… my… my dress… and… but…"

"But what? I've got you," Gwen kissed her forehead.

"Does Dave know?"

Gwen shrugged. "I don't know what the menfolk have up their sleeves but they have very specific time restraints."

"I'm getting married today?" Evelynn cried.

"You are…" Gwen kissed her head and hugged her again. "But… I really need you to stop crying… we're on a schedule, sister…"

Evelynn laughed and nodded, blowing her nose and taking in a deep breath giving in to the process.

Gwen darted in and out of the room, disappearing for long moments at a time. Evelynn was thankful that there were snacks on hand when her bacon and eggs from breakfast no longer held her over. She sat on the stool sipping champagne mixed with orange juice in her robe from her office. There was a glitch in Gwen's plans and Evelynn tried not to think on it. No one's better at planning events like that woman. If she said she "had it", then, she does.

As if she heard Evelynn's thoughts, the very person walked into the room texting madly on her phone. She stopped short when she spotted Evelynn looking at her. "Oh my..." Gwen smiled. "You look so beautiful."

Evelynn smiled sincerely. Her make-up was soft with brown's and blues making her dark colored eyes look almost black. Her hair was in a low bun with soft curls pinned and twisted all around it. A delicate twist of tiny pearls wound their way through the elegant design.

Gwen held up her hands, "Don't! Don't cry!" She could see Evelynn's eyes mist over and feared that a tear would slip away.

Evelynn in true theatre fashion, looked up and dabbed beneath her eye to catch any wayward tears from escaping.

"I'm here! I'm here!" Nina Black came running into the dressing room carrying a long garment bag above her head.

Evelynn looked at her confused.

"Oh, Evie, you look beautiful," she said pausing by a temporary clothes rack. "But I think something might be missing."

She hung the garment bag on the rack and unzipped the long zipper in the front.

Evelynn's jaw dropped when she saw the contents of the bag.

"I'm sorry we were running so late," Nina apologized, "I had to wait for the dry cleaners to put a rush on it!"

Peeking from inside the bag was the most delicate lace and beadwork Evelynn had ever seen. Nina slipped her arm underneath the length of the antique wedding dress allowing it to hang freely.

"Oh my goodness... is that...?"

Nina nodded. "It's the dress we found in the trunk of the Horsch. I had it dry cleaned for this once in a lifetime special occasion. I hope you don't mind."

"Mind? Oh, it's so beautiful! I don't even know what to say!"

"Well, don't say anything yet," Gwen interrupted her ogling. "Let's see if it fits first. If not, you may be getting married in your robe."

"Don't be silly," Gillian reminded, "We have several wedding gowns in the costume closet."

"No," Gwen stood back and looked at her very best friend putting on the dress that looked like it was made for her perfect dancer's body. "Those couldn't even compare to this one. This is absolutely perfect."

Chapter Eighteen

Gwen walked her best friend out to the lobby. Evelynn gasped when she rounded the corner.

There in the center of the lobby was a huge decorated Christmas tree. It reached up toward the ceiling and the star was blinking in different patterns of brilliant white lights. Huge colored ornaments hung daintily on the branches while lights and ribbons wove their way through the bows from top to bottom.

"Oh! Oh Gwen! It is SO beautiful!! You have done so much! How... how on earth... "

"The McCarty's... they brought it up and decorated it." She leaned against Evelynn and linked arms with her admiring the beautiful centerpiece for just a moment as the guests were taking their seats in the auditorium.

"Stay right here. I'll be right back." Gwen ordered.

Evelynn smiled, and nodded.

Gwen came back toward the lobby with a line of tiny ballerina's following her. "Evie?" Gwen whispered and stepped further into the lobby... "Evie?"

"I'm here." Evelynn called back.

Gwen gasped. "Evelynn St. Lawrence! What are you doing! You're going to be married any moment now!" Gwen looked down at the base of the Christmas tree to see Evelynn's stocking feet wiggling back and forth as she lay under the tree. Her wedding shoes were waiting patiently beside her, ready when she was.

Gwen couldn't help but laugh.

"Erin was right. This is an amazing view."

"Why are you under the tree, Miss Evie?"

"Who is that? Is that you, Chloe?"

She giggled. "Yup."

Evelynn scooted as daintily as she could to see the row of snowflake ballerinas standing in front of her snickering.

She smiled at them; their sweet, sweet faces.

"Come on..." Gwen whispered! "You're up!" She escorted the snowflakes to the auditorium door. They followed in their single file line, and bringing up the rear was Bella.

"You look pretty, Miss Evie," she stage whispered.

"Thank you, so do you." Evelynn couldn't stop smiling.

The tiny dancers filed their way toward the stage as the music played the *Snowflake Waltz* from the *Nutcracker*.

Gwen retreated back down the hallway toward the dressing room but before slipping through the door, she turned back saying, "Stay right there!"

The door to the auditorium was cracked ever so slightly allowing Evelynn a glimpse of the transformed stage. She could see a backdrop painted with a beautiful winter scene. Huge snow, covered pine trees, beside a creek that had iced over. A spray of sunshine pierced through the naked trees standing like sentinels guarding the quiet countryside. Obviously the work of Jeanne, their set designer. Evelynn blinked heavily to keep from crying; imagining how long it must have taken her to paint that on such short notice.

She leaned to see the auditorium seating. The back half was their regular seating decorated with large white and red paper flowers. The front rows had church pews in place where the damaged seating once was. Evelynn furrowed her brow in puzzlement at how so much was transformed.

Gwen came in from around the corner and tugged the bride away from the door.

"Get back! You can't be seen yet!" Gwen scolded.

She had changed her dress and wore a stunningly brilliant red satin floor length gown from the same era as the wedding dress.

"How did you find a 1920's ..." Evelynn began.

Gwen held up her hand to silence her and tugged at the front panel adjusting things.

"You look beautiful," Evelynn whispered. Gwen couldn't help but smile at the sincerity of Evelynn's compliment.

She walked over and gently hugged her. "You look beautiful. I hope this is okay."

Evelynn was silenced. No words would come to her to properly express how deeply she appreciated and was so amazed and impressed at everything her best friend had done for her to make this day happen.

"I couldn't have done better myself. I love it. I love everything. I love you."

"I love you too... so, so much."

Suddenly, the music changed and Gwen snapped to attention. "Oh! It's our turn! Where are your flowers?"

Evelynn just opened her empty hands, "I... don't... do I have flowers?"

Gwen took off running down the back hallway through the heavy backstage door, down the corridor to the dressing room. She grabbed a delicately designed bouquet of long stem medium white roses and red amaryllis, with seeded eucalyptus and Hypercom berry tucked in wrapped with a red, gold and lace ribbon, and high-tailed it back to the theatre door without breaking a sweat.

"You'll know your cue..." She took a long last look at her best friend, winked at her, and opened the door to walk down the center aisle.

Evelynn did her best not to cry as she watched her flawlessly gorgeous maid of honor walk down toward the stage which was now out of her view.

Her heart pounded in her chest as she imagined Gwen walking down each set of steps, across the base of the stage, up the side steps and into her place as Maid of Honor.

The music quieted and Evelynn shivered. *Is this really happening? This is my wedding day.*

Thank you, God, for everything that had to happen to get us here today. I thank you for never leaving my side, and for carrying me when I couldn't stand on my own. I thank you for these wonderful people you've put in my life and I..."

Suddenly, a string quartet began to play. Evelynn let them play an introduction, and then had to swallow the lump in her throat when she heard what they were playing. There were no vocals, but she sang the words quietly in her head, as she stepped through the auditorium doors.

At last, my love has come along... my lonely days are over, and life is like a song...

She walked across the back of the theatre behind the very back row of seats. As she came in, all of the guests were on their feet. She walked to the center aisle and stopped, not believing what was in front of her.

Strings of vintage Edison light bulbs zigzagged across the ceilings and rafters offering a soft glow. A few blinking white lights that were added to look like the stars, were winking down at her smiling with their approval. The gaping hole that was in the roof showed the deep blue hues of the setting sun and looked so perfect, one might have thought it was an extension of Jeanne's backdrop. The only clues that they were all standing in the place of a recent disaster was the slight chill in the air and the need for some to wear a wrap or light coat. Rose petals were tossed across the floor covering up the raw concrete and the church loaned seating for the first three rows of guests. Evelynn saw nothing of the flaws of the building or the amount of work in front of them to return it to its former glory: she was in her very own fairytale.

Evelynn's eyes dropped to the stage in front of her. In front of the amazing winter backdrop, a throne that was recently used in their version of *Camelot*, sat beside an archway decorated with tiny white lights and miniature rose flowers. Gwen stood beautifully to the left of the archway, holding a smaller bouquet. Sitting on the throne, was her husband to be. She could see that there was a walker leaning against the side of the chair. And Nick stood to the right of the (formerly King Arthur) throne.

She swallowed hard and looked at all of the people in attendance. Co-workers, students, parents, family and friends. Helen and Walter had made it back into town for the wedding. Helen had her coat wrapped tightly around her and looked up at the ceiling, scowling. Evelynn could only imagine what she was saying, but chose to not think about it. Walter however, smiled at her so warmly that Helen's scowl faded to the background.

Evelynn could barely contain her emotions.

You smiled, oh, and then the spell was cast, and here we are in heaven...

She forced herself to take a step toward the stage. And then another. She saw that a ramp had been built from the bottom row to center stage. She walked slowly toward the most perfect wedding she could have ever hoped for. On the front pew, Lucas stood crying. He flapped his handkerchief at her as she passed. She reached out and touched his arm, silently thanking him, knowing that the theatre's magical atmosphere was largely due to his talents and vision. He blew her kisses all the way up the ramp. She paused at the edge of the stage to take in the scene for just a few seconds more. She couldn't believe this was really happening.

Gwen met Evelynn at center stage and held out her hand guiding her to the left side of the glistening archway.

Gwen took a step behind Evelynn and nodded for her to face her groom.

Nick stepped forward and held out a hand for Dave to grab ahold of.

Dave took the outstretched hand and weakly stood to his feet. He looked at Evelynn and she could see the pain cross his face but the tears were for happiness. He took the couple steps toward his bride on his own and grabbed her hands so that they could face each other under the arch.

Evelynn raised her eyebrows in question, are you alright?

He scrunched his face in response and bobbed his shoulder, piece of cake.

The same pastor that baptized David Ripke at their church stood beside them to perform the ceremony to make them man and wife.

Because of Dave's stubbornness to stand through the entire ceremony, Pastor Rodgers decided to go with the shorter version.

They spoke the original vows, they exchanged rings and then...

"I now pronounce you husband and wife. You may kiss the bride."

A light snowfall fell on the newlyweds. As the guests oooh'd and ahhh'd and camera flashes caught the moment, Evelynn couldn't help but glance over at the first row, first seat, silently scolding. There, Lucas could only shrug his shoulders and dab at the tears in his eyes.

And just before Dave's weak legs were ready to give out on him they heard the sound of large jingle bells... the kind that horses wear.

Evelynn looked past her new husband and saw James leading a brilliant white horse pulling a two-seater sleigh. He rounded the sleigh behind the couple and stopped it right in front of them.

Nick helped Evelynn slide in the bench seat and cover up with a thick faux fur blanket and then gave Dave the strong arm to lift himself into the sleigh. Dave shook his head and laughed giving Lucas the thumbs up while Evelynn could only smile and roll her eyes. And with a crack of the reins, the glittery white horse took the newlyweds out the back door of the theatre.

... for you are mine, at last....

The End

A Simple Spring Wedding

It was a simple Sunday in Spring. Less than a dozen close family and friends were in attendance.

Way back at the end of the hay fields of the Penn property, a small wooded cove was opened up, and trimmed back ever so slightly to allow the small number of chairs and guests to witness the marriage between Nick Penn and Gwen Collins.

The tiny creek gurgled along happily with the string quartet that played, announcing the procession.

Evelynn Ripke walked under the all-natural canopy that was bent into an archway of sweet smelling white freesia, down the center aisle created by two rows of folding chairs.

The strings went quiet, building the anticipation.

From the back of the clearing, bride and groom walked down the center together, arm in arm as Pachelbel Cannon escorted them.

The guests rose in silent respect as the couple made their way to the alter.

Gwen was wearing an off-white satin gown that brushed the ground as she walked. On her head, she wore a crown of pink and purple boho flowers. Her hair was twisted up in curls and wrapped delicately around her flower crown. She cradled an assortment of pink, purple and orange tulips cut from their own yard, wrapped in strips of lace binding the bouquet together in the crook of her arm.

They faced each other in front of a small water fountain that Nick put in earlier that month. It drew from the creek and spilled out over delicate edges and greenery making it the perfect backdrop for their vows.

Pastor Rodgers stepped forward and instructed the guests to be seated.

"Before we can begin our wedding ceremony today, we must add a special segment at the request of the groom." He turned to Nick and nodded.

Gwen looked at the front row and smiled at Erin sitting next to Judy, Gwen's mother. She reached out her hand for Erin to join her. Erin grinned and blushed slightly before moving next to her.

Nick bent down on one knee in front of the child and produced a box from his front pocket. "Erin, I hope you know that I think the world of you and your mom. So much so, that I want you both in my life forever. Would you please accept this gift from your mother and I, and say that we can be a family?"

He opened the box and inside glistened the most delicate blue stone in the center of a gold cross ring.

Erin giggled but nodded her head. She looked up at her mother who was fighting to hold back tears. Gwen nodded, and Erin held out her hand so that Nick could place the ring on her finger. He leaned in and kissed the back of her hand. Erin was so filled with emotion that she started crying and clung to Nick's neck. "I love you, Daddy."

"I love you too, baby girl." He lifted her in his arms so the three could embrace. "Would you mind if I marry your mom now?"

Erin laughed, "Yeah, I guess so." She wriggled free of his embrace and made her way back to her seat, "You guys can go ahead now..." she waved them along as if they were holding things up.

Gwen was already crying when Nick returned to face her. He wiped away her tears with his thumb and smiled at her. It was the most beautiful face she had ever seen and finally, they were going to be together.

"Dearly beloved, we are gathered here today..."

A Simple Summer Wedding

Hay bales created the perfect geometric design for seating and a small alter in the backyard of Gillian Sanders. A huge white tent would shield guests from the scorching sun during the wedding and, when the hay bales were removed, for dancing in the evening.

Cattle lined the fences wanting to be a part of the excitement in the air. Children ran in all directions. Flavorful smoke wafted from the three barbeque grills that lined the back porch. Long tables decorated with bright colorful tablecloths and bouquets of Gerber daisies waited for guests to fill them.

Music filled the air as the final preparations were put into place. In her bedroom, Gillian looked at herself one last time in the mirror. Her white calf-length wedding dress came off her shoulders and gathered in a puff of pinched fabric. A bright yellow headband matched the bow in the back of her dress.

Her maid of honor, Rae, had just finished the final touches of her hair and dashed out to get herself ready.

Following a soft knock on the door, her grown twin daughters entered her bedroom.

"Mom, we are so happy for you, "Michelle said gently, hugging her.

"Yeah," Rebecca agreed. "This is right. Tom is a good match for you."

Tears welled up in Gillian's eyes. "That means so much to hear that from you. I wanted so much for you to like him. He's not going to replace..."

"We know."

"I'm sorry, it took me so long to see..."

Gillian shook her head, "No... no... it's okay." She pulled them both close to her and they huddled, foreheads touching, the same way they have been embracing each other for years. "I'm so glad that you are here. Where's my grand-girl?"

"She's outside running with Ethan and the other kids. If she messes up that dress..."

"Then we'll just wipe it off."

"You look amazing, mom. Really. You do."

"Thank you, my girls. I am very happy."

"It shows."

"Momma!"   Allie came in through the screen door at the side of Gillian's bedroom. She was dressed in a smaller version of Gillian's dress and carried a basket of artificial flowers, which she dangled and twirled as if it was a purse.

"Yes, honey?"

"Ethan won't stop jumping off the hay seats. He's messing them up. And..." she jutted out her hip, "He took off his tie." She rolled her eyes, exasperated.

Gillian smiled calmly at her suffering. "Where is Shurita? She's supposed to be here with you."

"She said that the shoes were hurting her feet and she'll wait until it's time to fix stuff."

"Well, could you please go and get her and tell her that it's time?"

"It's time? Really?"

"Pretty close."

Allie ran back out the door and then back in picking up her basket that she had left on the bed... and back out.

A tap was heard at the door.

Anthony, Gillian's father, poked his head in the room. "Are we about ready? Your mother needs to get out of the kitchen before the entire catering staff walks out," He slipped into the room and jerked his head toward the back yard, "and if your groom keeps tugging at his collar much longer, it's going to come off!"

Gillian smiled, imagining her handsome groom in his military uniform, waiting for permission to get back to his jeans and t-shirt.

She spun one last time in the mirror and Michelle adjusted the bright yellow bow in the back of her dress.

They heard the music pause and the D.J. speak softly into the microphone requesting that the guests make their way to their seats.

Gillian took in a deep breath. A lot of healing had to happen before this day. She was proud of the person she had become and looked forward to the next phase of her life, with this man she deeply loved... and, who loved her back. Maybe the next years won't be as stressful. She laughed quietly to herself.

She smiled at her image in the mirror and linked her arm with her father's, "I'm definitely ready," Gillian smiled.

Acknowledgements:

Barbara Bourgeret- My momma. Always first on my mind and heart to acknowledge; because without her love and support (and cramming my books down people's throats) who knows where I'd be? Her love for me is unwavering and her belief in me never dims. If only every child were so lucky as to have the support system such as I.

Amber Simon- One of my brilliant Bonus Children who patiently helped me though medically induced comas and burn traumas perfectly willing to relay details to me at any given hour of the day or night. (You never know when I'm going to get stuck!)   So proud of this girl and all she has accomplished in the medical field and grateful that she was willing to share her knowledge and texts with me.

Jan Kelley- the newest member of my team, my promotion's executive. I am so honored that someone else out there (other than my mother) believes in me and the work that I do; so much so that she has chosen to help me build my platform and hopefully get my books and workshops in front of new eyes. I love her already and I believe that we can build beautiful things together.

Pat Lambert- My editor. Her red marks are always followed by smiles and words of encouragement... it's impossible to get upset at that. I am so very grateful for your hours of tedious reading and re-reading so I don't look like and uneducated idiot. Lol!

Sometimes you meet just the right people at the time when you need them most. That goes for these folks who were strangers before the writing of this book and yet have played an integral part in its creation.

Don Crum-my boating expert- he gave me the play by play so I could bring you the most realistic boating accident.

Sarahi Robles- my Spanish amiga. She was so kind as to translate my words into Spanish to bring Carlos to life.

Roxanne Taylor- google specialist extraordinaire-ready with a few clicks and the internet to fill in those last minute gaps and details I was needing.

Aaron Bower- special thanks to my very good friend who gave me insight (sometimes unintentionally) into character development.

Thank you to my readers. You have built Bakersfield and have grown it into a place full of great memories. I have truly enjoyed your feedback and love and support for this series and hope the stories and characters bring you back to Bakersfield again and again.

It's hard to say good-bye to a series, now that I've gotten attached but the other stories that are rattling around in my head are begging to be told and I feel the need to yield to their urging. I hope the new cast of characters will be accepted into your hearts.

I am so grateful that God has not only given me a gift of words, but the opportunity to share them. I am blessed more that I deserve and am forever grateful for his grace and forgiveness.

Check out the new section of my website devoted to Bakersfield!
You can find all the books and even some unique gift ideas! Who doesn't need Bakersfield Swag??
www.elizabethbourgeret.com